A burst o   glass tinkled from
the hall's shattered windows. Riders were charging up and
down the flat, shooting at any and everything.

Slocum pressed the girl down and pulled on his pants, then
his boots.

"Who are they?" she asked.

"White men, I imagine. Stay low." He was up and gone.
More than anything, he wanted to interrogate one of them, so
he could learn who was the leader.

"Sumbitch, they ain't here!" someone cussed out in front
when Slocum made the back of the building. The six-gun in
his hand, he edged himself for the corner.

"Wiley's right, there ain't no Injuns here."

"The sumbitch tricked us."

Slocum moved down the side and reached the corner. His
gun was cocked and ready.

"Hands high or die." Six-guns belched red-orange flames,
others struck on empty. His first shot was at the figure standing on the porch who screamed he was hit. Then Slocum shot
at the outline on the horse. That one dropped his pistol on the
ground. His panicked horse spun out from beneath him and
spilled him on the ground. The rest of the gang raced out of
camp. A raider on the ground had not moved, but Slocum
thought he might not be playing possum.

"Who's your dead friend?" he asked the blanch-faced cowboy.

Yost never answered. Filled with anger, Slocum grasped the
cowboy by his vest and jerked him off the ground.

"Answer me. Was Leo Krier here tonight?"

DON'T MISS THESE
ALL-ACTION WESTERN SERIES
FROM THE BERKLEY PUBLISHING GROUP

THE GUNSMITH by J. R. Roberts
Clint Adams was a legend among lawmen, outlaws, and ladies. They called him . . . the Gunsmith.

LONGARM by Tabor Evans
The popular long-running series about Deputy U.S. Marshal Long—his life, his loves, his fight for justice.

SLOCUM by Jake Logan
Today's longest-running action Western. John Slocum rides a deadly trail of hot blood and cold steel.

BUSHWHACKERS by B. J. Lanagan
An action-packed series by the creators of Longarm! The rousing adventures of the most brutal gang of cutthroats ever assembled—Quantrill's Raiders.

DIAMONDBACK by Guy Brewer
Dex Yancey is Diamondback, a Southern gentleman turned con man when his brother cheats him out of the family fortune. Ladies love him. Gamblers hate him. But nobody pulls one over on Dex . . .

WILDGUN by Jack Hanson
The blazing adventures of mountain man Will Barlow—from the creators of Longarm!

TEXAS TRACKER by Tom Calhoun
Meet J.T. Law: the most relentless—and dangerous—manhunter in all Texas. Where sheriffs and posses fail, he's the best man to bring in the most vicious outlaws—for a price.

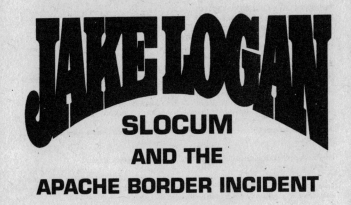

SLOCUM

AND THE

APACHE BORDER INCIDENT

J

JOVE BOOKS, NEW YORK

THE BERKLEY PUBLISHING GROUP
Published by the Penguin Group
Penguin Group (USA) Inc.
375 Hudson Street, New York, New York 10014, USA
Penguin Group (Canada), 90 Eglinton Avenue East, Suite 700, Toronto, Ontario M4P 2Y3, Canada
(a division of Pearson Penguin Canada Inc.)
Penguin Books Ltd., 80 Strand, London WC2R 0RL, England
Penguin Group Ireland, 25 St. Stephen's Green, Dublin 2, Ireland (a division of Penguin Books Ltd.)
Penguin Group (Australia), 250 Camberwell Road, Camberwell, Victoria 3124, Australia
(a division of Pearson Australia Group Pty. Ltd.)
Penguin Books India Pvt. Ltd., 11 Community Centre, Panchsheel Park, New Delhi—110 017, India
Penguin Group (NZ), Cnr. Airborne and Rosedale Roads, Albany, Auckland 1310, New Zealand
(a division of Pearson New Zealand Ltd.)
Penguin Books (South Africa) (Pty.) Ltd., 24 Sturdee Avenue, Rosebank, Johannesburg 2196,
South Africa

Penguin Books Ltd., Registered Offices: 80 Strand, London WC2R 0RL, England

This is a work of fiction. Names, characters, places, and incidents either are the product of the author's imagination or are used fictitiously, and any resemblance to actual persons, living or dead, business establishments, events, or locales is entirely coincidental.

SLOCUM AND THE APACHE BORDER INCIDENT

A Jove Book / published by arrangement with the author

PRINTING HISTORY
Jove edition / June 2006

ISBN: 0-515-14143-7

JOVE®
Jove Books are published by The Berkley Publishing Group,
a division of Penguin Group (USA) Inc.,
375 Hudson Street, New York, New York 10014.
JOVE is a registered trademark of Penguin Group (USA) Inc.
The "J" design is a trademark belonging to Penguin Group (USA) Inc.

PRINTED IN THE UNITED STATES OF AMERICA

10 9 8 7 6 5 4 3 2 1

Prologue

Billie Barton hitched up her too-big men's pants by the buckle, then fought the long sleeves on the shirt up so her hands could appear. Where had Fred gone? In the hustle and bustle of this railroad boomtown they called Deming, she'd lost her husband. That man. Off on one of his money-making schemes that always ended the same—in the dust.

Hot wind swept her face and tussled her short dark hair. She must be a sight, but she never cared how she looked. That was for vain, fancy women. All her nineteen years she'd been more boy than girl anyway. Except for those inconveniences that her female body shared with all dress-wearers like periods and squatting to pee, she was a boy and proud of it.

In the ill-fitting brogan, she shuffled along, searching both sides of the busy street. Besides, Fred liked her just like she was—it was why she married him. Most fellars would have wanted her to wear a dress and be prissy. Not her way.

She stopped and studied the dark-skinned men standing around wrapped in blankets. That must be hot. Did they have clothes on under them? She had known some grown boys back in Arkansas that were so poor all they owned for clothes was a night shirt.

Those blanket-wearing men looked dusty and their hair was in braids tied with fluttering rags. If they were the Apaches people talked about . . . no, they were mean and killed folks. That bunch of stuffed blankets looked too stiff to do anything that hard.

Where was Fred? She ran her tongue over her upper gums

where she'd lost her four top front teeth in the wagon wreck. Inconvenient, but they were gone. Made her look funny in a looking glass, but what could she do? She didn't have any more to fill in the gap and she could put whatever in the corner of her mouth and gnaw it off. Shucks, her eighty-some-year-old granny had no teeth at all and was still alive back in Texas.

Texas. Shame that Fred hated the place. Farmland wasn't bad around Sherman. But no, Fred wanted to see San Antonio. Well, San Anton was like this place. If you didn't speak Spanish you needed to learn how—no one spoke English. And the hill country down there wasn't the answer. No sir, not for Fred. He was going to get rich in California.

When her and her six brothers loaded their wagon and headed out of Madison County, Arkansas, she'd thought Texas would be her home forever. Not knowing how a girl could be fooled. A train of ten wagons and some stragglers riding along all headed off the Boston Mountains into the Indian Nation on the old Butterfield Road. Fred must have joined them at Fort Smith. He showed up around then anyway.

Fred must have been in his mid-twenties. He had a medium build, wore store-bought wool pants and a pullover shirt, galluses, a vest and a cowboy hat. She took him for a cowboy. But later, he'd told her he found the outfit out on the prairie, west of the Fort. And she never knew undertakers sold clothes, but she learned later, too, that was how Fred got his outfit—some Texas drover who'd brought cattle up there had died. He wore a pocket watch that didn't work, too. For months, she thought the thing was ticking away.

"What time is it?" she would ask him at midday break.

He'd fish it out, snap open the lid and say, "Twelve-fifteen."

Satisfied she knew the exact moment in her world, she went off doing the things necessary to make her crew some dinner. Her brothers, Matthew, Mark, Luke, John, Paul, and Caesar, all took to him. Fred could tell some tall tales and he had some big plans. Her brothers, raised in the mountains on a hardscrabble farm, had no ideas about making money besides raising crops and hunting small game to eat. Fred had enough schemes for four families. But then they sounded fresh. The Neals had struck out to find a better way to live. Besides what was one more mouth to feed? They were so busy listening to Fred's grand plans they never noticed he didn't contribute anything to the food pot. But it wasn't necessary. Mat and Mark could bring in squirrels, rabbits, possums, coons or fish enough to feed an army. They rode bareback on some horses they'd traded for before leaving home and swung out to find game every day.

Being good hunters, they shared their bounty with others like her Uncle Dolphin and his wife Cyd who cared for her Granny Neal. The time was fall and the summer's heat had evaporated. Hardwoods hadn't turned yet when they went through the mountains in the Injun Nation; the country was lots similar to the hills back home. Every day was a picnic for her. New sights, a new campground, and they were going to what Ruff Hackberry called the land of plenty. Ruff was the wagon boss.

She'd begun to notice Fred looking at her a lot after he'd found out she wasn't a boy. Must have took him a week to learn the truth and before he knew what she was, he had amused her when he jumped up and peed a big stream in front of her. She wanted to laugh at how he arched his hips forward and held his dick in his hand like something precious before he let fly.

One evening she came around the wagon in the dark and ran into him. He threw his arms around her, lifted her up and before she could bat an eye, kissed her on the mouth. His move caught her by such surprise it dazzled her into a stupor.

"I been looking all my life for a woman just like you to share my life," he whispered in her ear.

Those words to her were like the song in the windup music box. They swept her away and him holding her pressed to him, her feet off the ground, she felt like she was flying. And instead of having a wild cat fit, she fluffed up his sideburns and looked into his big green eyes—damn that suited her better than anything ever had before. She threw her arms around him and went to kissing him back like she was possessed.

Under the onslaught of her mouth and weight, Fred staggered backwards and fell over the wagon tongue. Spilt both of them on the grass. On top of him, she swept his hair back from his forehead and looked at him, worried.

"You all right?"

"Sure, darling. Long as I got you, I'll be fine."

So the courtship of Billie Neal began, started somewheres around Foggy Bottoms Depot, Injun Nation. Wasn't long before

Fred was fondling her tender breasts when they kissed behind the wagon or a tree. That hurt, but she guessed if the likes made her man happy she could stand the pain. Besides she wasn't noticing much of anything but Fred. One morning she even forgot to put the scorched barley in the boiling water to make coffee and went to pouring out clear hot water in their cups. Sure made her face red with all them boys geehaffing at her forgetfulness. Good thing they had the Neal good-naturedness. Why, someone like Ruff Hackberry would have had a mad fit over his wife doing a forgetful thing like that.

Then one warm evening, Fred held his finger to his lips and led her away from camp. It was before the moon came up and the stars were just popping out.

"Where we going?" she hissed at him.

"Don't you never mind, I've got a big surprise for you."

What the heck, she was with him and that was all she cared about. So she pulled up her pants to keep from walking on the hem and pushed back her sleeves, then hurried to keep up. They were at last far enough from everyone and he stopped.

"You know all about boys, don't ya?" he asked.

"Sure they got things like stud horses."

"Good. Cause with us getting all serious, I didn't want to scare you."

"Scare me?" She looked around in the night full of the sounds of sissy bugs. What was he getting at? She knew all about sex; she'd watched horses breed mares a hundred times. Even seen through a knothole in the shed her own oldest brother breeding Molly Sims in the hay. Course at the time, she thought it was damn nice of Mat to save her husband all that hard work. It sure done in that sorrel stallion when he screwed a mare, so it must exhaust a man bad, too.

His arm around her shoulder, Fred went on talking. "Sometimes the first time a woman sees something like it, she screams at the size of it. You know what I mean?"

"You're saying yours is real big, huh?"

"Big as they make 'em." He cupped her face in his hands. "Oh, my darling, you understand. You promise you won't scream at the sight of it?"

"I promise."

In big flurry, he went to pushing off his suspenders and

dropped his pants so his white legs shone in the starlight. She could make out his dick and it sure was no stud horse size, but she guessed it was big as they came. He said so anyway.

"Now if you'll get on your knees—"

Why? She'd seen it and didn't need to see it up closer than that. But she submitted when she put his hand on her shoulders and pushed her downward until she knelt in front of him.

"Now we've got to be real careful of him. You put him in your mouth and suck on him."

Suck on him? The notion made her stomach turn. Nobody ever mentioned doing this. Must be a real secret deal.

"You go ahead darling. You'll like it. Go ahead, real easy." One hand was behind her head pulling her toward the half stiff object while the other guided her face to it.

She parted her lips and her first taste of him was a strong fishy flavor. Then she grasped the shaft so he didn't gag her to death with the damn thing. In minutes, his tallywhacker ballooned to a much larger size and he was hunching it toward her. Then her brain began to swirl and she became totally inebriated on the job of sucking off the head of his dick. Her hand on the shaft soon found his scrotum and first chance she got, she squeezed both his nuts.

Fred gave a great gasp and his dick turned into a fountain of hot cum that filled her mouth and threatened to choke her to death. She broke away and bent over, spitting and coughing until she thought she'd puke.

"Oh, darling, oh darling. You all right?" He was on his knees hugging and squeezing her shoulder. "You're the best. The very best."

Regaining her breath at last, she nodded and wiped the tears away. She buried her face in his vest and hugged him. Like his breast squeezing, she guessed after that she could add dick sucking to a new list of thing she must put up with to have her a man.

On their wedding night, they honeymooned in an old shack about a mile from the farm the boys had rented outside of Sherman. It was Christmas Eve and Fred's present came in the box between her thighs. She never had no wedding dress. She never wore a dress no how. And she was excited the whole half-mile walk from the boys' farm after the preacher said, "You're husband and wife."

Fred, he couldn't wait. They had cake and nice things the neighbors brought them. No time for that. He quick-like led her down the dark, dusty road in the cold wind. She figured they'd freeze to death up there cause he'd never made no provisions for a stove.

Inside the old shack, she could see the stars out the cracks in the side walls and hugged her arms to keep warm.

"Get undressed," he said, busy stripping off his clothes like a madman about to jump in a swimming hole.

"It's too cold in here." She looked around all worried-like. First night she was married and she and her new husband would die of the cold. Even before he bred her. Lordy, Granny said it would be tough, but she expected nothing like this. At last in surrender she sat on the floor and undid her brogans.

"It won't be cold under all the covers," Fred kept promising her.

At last with her arms and back prickled with goose bumps and her shivering like a dying calf in a hail storm, she slipped naked into Fred's equally icy arms and against his frozen body. He rocked her, kissed her and then clumsy as she ever saw him, he managed to get his dick half in her and came.

She closed her eyes as he mumbled about being too excited. This was supposed to be something special—their evening—and instead she was freezing to death with goo all inside her legs and running out of her like a leaky bucket. There weren't enough covers in Texas to keep her warm either.

That moment, she made up her mind then and there, she'd have to do more of the planning in their lives. Fred was a dreamer and he always thought the situation would all work out—some how.

Fred got better at sex and she liked it much more than having his pecker stuck in her mouth. Except he'd have to have some at the most awkward times. They'd be all packed up to move on and he'd want to go have some. It disrupted her mind, but she went along cause he was always gentle, never mad at her even if the whole thing didn't go so good. Billie had seen the black side of Ruff Hackberry toward his wife over little things and figured she had a much better man in Fred than him.

About that very moment, she saw him coming down the boardwalk with an armload of supplies. Hat on the back of his head and a big smile. How could she be mad at him over that?

"I got the things we need to go to California now," he said.

"You sure it's enough?" She jerked up her pants and hurried to keep up with him.

"Sure, we can get on our horses and ride."

"How far is it? Did you ask?"

"The other side of Arizona and we're better'n half way across New Mexico now."

That wasn't the distance they'd gone, but hell, Fred was never bothered with details—they just worked out.

So they left Deming and the end of the Southern Pacific tracks to follow what Fred assured her was the thirty-year-old Butterfield Stage trail. Sure enough some stages passed them.

But it was dry flat desert country and when they saw the mountains in the distance, she daydreamed about Arkansas. He rambled on about making a steamboat that could walk and carry folks across the desert without rails since they had learned in Deming that the Southern Pacific was out of money for building any more track. But she never heard much of his latest scheme; it went by her like the wind that blew all the time out there and carried sharp pieces of sand.

That night they camped near a stage stop called Steins. The next morning they'd saddled their horses and were about to break camp, when Fred slipped up behind her, hugged her and bent over kissing her neck. She'd taught him to go easy on her breasts, so she let him undo a blouse button, shove his hand in and feel the left one. Oh, well—

With the bedroll from off her saddle under her arm, she led her lovesick husband to the mesquite thicket under the hill. She sat on the bedroll and removed her brogans. Fred was toeing off his boots and breathing harder than a runaway horse as he undressed. When she stood up and shed her pants, the cool morning wind swept her bare legs and butt.

Fred wasted no time getting on his knees; his dong was waving like a flagpole. On her back, legs parted for him, she smiled, pleased. He loved her and had been like this for eighteen months. Her eyes closed, she felt him slip it inside her and begin to pound away. Her breath quickened and she raised her butt to accept more of him. She liked it, she liked it a lot—then she heard something going on near the horses.

"What's that?" Fred shouted and his dick came out of her. He scrambled to his feet to go see about them.

"Fred, where's your gun?" she hissed.

"I traded it for food in Deming." He waved away her concern and charged off.

She closed her eyes.

"Indians!" he cried out and to her dismay started for them.

"No!" She scrambled to try to catch him, but he was gone running bare-ass up there to stop them. "Fred! Let 'em have them!"

She reached the top of the bank in time to see two near naked Indians leading off their horses. Her scream to make her husband not try to do anything never came out of her throat. Instead, riding past him, the second Indian aimed a large revolver point-blank down at Fred. The gun exploded in a cloud of black smoke and Fred staggered to a stop, holding his chest with both hands. His snow white legs shone in the sunlight as they crumbled underneath him. She knew her husband was dead.

1

A gray wool blanket was spread on the ground in the lacy shade of the mesquite tree. Three men played cards on it. One of them was Army Captain Oliver Blake, a tall lean-built man with a mustache and small dark eyes that desert duty had burned out. His uniform coat unbuttoned, his tie undone, Blake was on his knees looking hard at his five-card hand.

Squatting across from Blake was Curly Madison, a former army scout who was in his thirties. Madison sported brown hair to his shoulders, a buckskin pullover shirt glazed with dirt and sweat and black-striped gray woolen pants tucked in knee-high stub-toed boots. He hadn't shaved in a week and one whiff of his body odor confirmed that he hadn't bathed in a lot longer time. With his swarthy complexion, Madison might have been part Messikin, but Slocum wasn't certain.

Dressed in canvas pants and suspenders, Slocum wore a puffy-sleeved, pullover cotton shirt with a wool vest and a good beaver hat cocked back on his head. Intent upon the game, he studied his fellow cardplayers for any facial clues, then looked hard at the five cards in his hand.

"Raise you a dollar," Blake said, somber-faced as a judge.

"Ain't worth it," Slocum said and tossed his cards on the blanket.

"I'll see that and one more," Madison said. He threw in two silver cartwheels that clunked on the other money in the center.

9

Slocum noticed a kid coming toward them. Dressed in way-too-big pants and sleeves a yard too long, with unkempt dark brown hair, the kid crossed the bare ground, fighting all the time with the hem of the pants or the too-long sleeves.

"You winning?" the kid asked Slocum, with one hand jerking up the pants and the other fighting up the surplus sleeve that threatened to swallow his hands.

In a glance, Slocum saw the kid had no front teeth. Eye teeth showed on both sides. Just some riffraff youngster hanging around a stage station on the day they were trying to repair the coach's right rear wheel.

"Whats'cher name kid?" Madison asked, looking up from his hand.

A curl of lip, head drawn back, the youth spoke. "I ain't no damn kid. I'm a grown woman."

"You sure as hell didn't grow much." Madison chuckled.

"Lay off of her," Slocum said, realizing perhaps there *was* a young woman under that oversized garb.

"You got a husband?" Madison asked, swiveling on the toes of his boots and making an obscene knowing-all face at her.

"Not no more."

"Where'd he go?"

"The sumbitch's died."

"You kill him?"

"Naw, but I should have."

"Aw, maybe you want to make a dollar real quick-like, huh?"
She blinked at the scout. "What for?"

"We go over in the arroyo and do this." He used his index finger to run in and out of the circle of the other one.

"I ain't no damn *puta*," she said, affronted-sounding, and turned on her men's brogan heels to hike back to the stage depot.

"I'd give you two dollars," Madison shouted, but his words fell on deaf ears as she tugged and stumbled along across the caliche ground.

"You going to screw orphans or play?" Blake asked, sounding irritated by the delay.

"I would screw that one." Madison raised up and looked after her some more.

"Two aces," Blake said.

"Oh—" Madison still was watching after her. "Three fives."

"Sumbitch," Blake swore at the scout. "You'd screw a goat if someone would keep the horns out of your belly."

"He already has," Slocum said and picked up the cards to shuffle them. "Wonder if they'll get that wheel repaired or not this afternoon?"

"Damned if I know," Blake said, and sat down cross-legged on the ground.

Madison did the same thing and shook his head. "I never screwed a damn goat. Sheep, that is different."

"Aw, crap, who in the hell would ever screw a sheep?"

Madison looked up at the sky. "You've never been real horny? Sheep, they ain't so bad."

"Well," Blake said, looking at his new hand, "if I had I'd damn sure never brag about it."

"There you see you are an officer and a gentlemen. I am a simple sheep-fucker."

"Gawdamnit, what the hell are you going to do?" Slocum demanded.

"Oh, it is my turn to open." The ex-scout looked hard at his new cards, curled his lip and threw them down. "No three of a kind in that one."

Blake shut his eyes, then shook his head in dismay. "That's why they call it draw poker."

"Can't you feel the cards? They talk to me and say you don't have nothing and won't get nothing."

"Cards don't talk, you idiot."

"Maybe not to an officer, but they talk to me."

"I hate to interrupt the game," said Buckskin Fuller, the driver, coming across the open ground. "We can't fix the wheel and there ain't a spare."

Busy cleaning his hands on a rag, he shook his head. "So I guess we'll spend the night here."

"It'll be three days for the next west-bound one, won't it?" Slocum asked.

"That's right. Be one here about noon tomorrow goes back to Lordsburg."

"But I need to report to Fort Grant," Blake said, sounding concerned.

"Can't help it," Fuller said.

"Hell, the damn army's waited this long, waiting three days

for you ain't no problem," Slocum said. "Now are we playing card or aren't we?"

"Nothing else to do." Blake shook his head with a sour look after Fuller.

They played until the agent's squaw came out and beat on a tub with a big spoon.

Slocum looked in her direction and nodded. "She must have lunch ready."

"I was ready to fold anyway."

"Wait, wait," Madison said.

"You get the ante," Slocum said and tossed in his cards.

"Damn, just when I had a real hand." The ex-scout threw down his cards and raked in the money. "What's for lunch?"

"Frijoles, so you can fart some more." Blake shook his head at the situation and got up.

"I keep telling you, I ain't no gentleman." Putting his winnings in his pocket with a jingle, Madison laughed at them. "But I can beat you two at cards."

"Today," Slocum said, removing his hat and wiping his damp forehead on his sleeve. Lady Luck went back and forth sooner or later. Better ride her to death when she was on your side. He checked the midday sun time and pulled down his hat. Whatever she had for them to eat, they'd better enjoy it since it sounded like they were going to be at this outpost for a while.

Inside the adobe hovel, Fuller sat at the long table with his plate heaped high in beans and stringy meat. He was using a flour tortilla to wrap up his lunch and smiled when he saw Slocum.

"Sorry about the damn wheel."

"No problem," Madison said, and stretched his arms over his head in the doorway. "I will win all their money at cards."

Slocum nodded when the woman handed him a plate of food and a cup of coffee. *"Gracias."*

"I have plenty more," she said and reached for the next plate full on her counter.

Slocum slid in on the end and soon found he had to move down—the ragamuffin slid in beside him.

"You not eating?" he asked.

She shook her head and raised her arms to expose her hands.

Then she put her elbows on the tabletop to hold back the excess fabric. Clasping her hands, she made a face. "I ain't hungry."

"I could buy you lunch."

She turned her head sideways and frowned at him. "Thought you were losing."

He chuckled in his throat. "Not that much."

She glanced over at the woman handing Blake his food. "I'll take one, too, Rosie." Then she nodded toward Slocum. "He's buying."

Then she turned back. "They call me Billie."

"Slocum," he said and loaded a fresh brown-specked tortilla with the bean-meat mixture.

"You got a wife?"

"No, why?"

"Just wondered." She looked around the room like a trapped bird wanting to escape.

"What happened to your husband?"

"Oh, him. Well, we were camped not far from here. Some Injun started stealing our horses and pack mule. Fred, he jumped up hollering at them." She dropped her chin and shook her head. "I tried to tell him they'd kill us."

"And?"

"When he ran over there to stop them that other Apache leveled his pistol at him and bang—shot him. Fred was dead and they still had the damn horses. That man was stupid. Now he's dead."

"Were you married long?"

She shook her head and took the plate of food that Rosie brought her. Slocum chewed on his and watched her. Like he suspected, she was starved and dug in to eat it.

In between bites, she waved her tortilla at him. "I married him on the wagon train coming from Arkansas to Texas, oh, maybe over a year ago. Texas never suited him, so we set out for California—"

She ate some more, then with a mouth full, continued. "He knew the way. Follow your face stupid, he told me. "Well, I did after they took it all and killed him. Then I finally got this far."

"Horses—" Madison said and jumped up from the far end of the bench to go and see.

Slocum watched the ex-scout go for his handgun and then rose himself, exchanging a questioning frown with Blake. Something was wrong and he wanted to see the source.

Old man Posey, who ran the stage stop, came bustling out of the kitchen in an apron and carrying a double-barrel shotgun. "I'll handle it," Posey said, walking past Madison and out under the palm-frond porch. He began talking in guttural Apache to the buck on the gray horse with the single eagle feather in his hair. Both men sounded tough from where Slocum could hear them out the open window. No doubt "eagle feather" was some kind of chief or subchief.

"What's he want, Posey?" Madison asked, when the speaking between the two slowed down.

"Wants some ammunition."

"Hell, we ain't got any of that," Madison said.

"Probably use it on us if we gave him any," Fuller said.

Slocum noticed Billie trying to look at all the horses and the bare-chested riders milling around behind the chief.

"See a pony that looks like yours?" Slocum asked in a whisper.

"Hell, no, but I'd bet a couple of them red bastards were the ones killed Fred."

"Give me a•half-dozen cartridges," Posey said, holding his hand out at them.

"What the fuck for?" Fuller asked with a frown at the rest of them.

"A gift of good faith. I've got to live with these people. His women sell me hay."

"Well, all right." The driver dug two out of his gun belt loops, Slocum did the same and Blake put two in, too.

"What about you?" the captain asked the ex-scout.

"I ain't a gentleman. That sumbitch is Gray Fox out there. I ain't giving him shit." Madison's eyes drew into narrow strips of glaring hatred.

Blake shook his head at Posey—obviously that was all they were donating.

Fuller put the half-dozen brass shells in Posey's hand. The depot man nodded and stepped off the porch. Slocum watched him walk over and put the cartridges in the chief's hand.

Gray Fox nodded in approval at the gift and spoke to Posey,

something inaudible to those in the room. Then Fox screamed so shrill, he drew goose bumps on the back of Slocum's arms despite the heat. Fox's brown-skinned bucks did the same, raising their rifles in the air, but not firing them. Slocum decided ammo was too precious for that exercise.

He turned and looked down at Billie standing close behind him, gnawing on a knuckle. She raised her gaze at him and her blue eyes looked like deep dark pools. A wave of upset went through her shoulders and caused her head to shake. She acted relieved when she saw them leave on their dancing ponies.

"They're going now. No trouble this time," he said to reassure her.

"That stupid Fred . . . I told him don't . . . let them have those horses. We could get more—but no! He had to run out there and challenge them." She looked out the window like something in the heat waves and far off Chiricahuas was holding her interest. "He never thought about me—being out there alone when they kilt him."

"They bother you."

She shook her head, still in a daze. "They just rode off with them animals. I stayed hid till I was sure they was gone."

"Tough deal for anyone."

"Tough was piling rocks on Fred, so the wolves wouldn't eat him. I could stand a lot, but not wolves gnawing on him." She held out her small palms for him to see. Scratched and skinned, they looked like they'd been attacked by a fighting cock.

"You going to wait for the next stage?" she asked.

Slocum nodded. "I imagine I will unless I can find some other transportation out of here."

"I guess I'd better try to find me a horse."

"Which way are you going? East or west?"

She scratched the dark thatch on the back of her head and wrinkled her small nose at him. "I can't decide. Go back to Texas or on to California."

"You have any gear left?"

"Naw, they took it all."

Three days in the outpost wasn't his idea of fun and good times. Besides he never knew when some bounty hunter had caught a scent of him and was coming up his back trail. On the move, he could duck and dart. He planned to buy a ticket to Yuma at Tucson, get off at Papago Wells and take the Prescott Stage north.

"There's a mining town south of here. We can get some horses there."

She looked hard up at him. "You asking me to go along?"

"No strings attached."

Suspicion spread over her face. "You done bought my dinner."

"Two bits—" He chuckled. "Why I lost more than that to Madison in the card game."

"But a horse costs big money." She looked around, but the others were over with Fuller on the other end of the room talking about the Apaches.

"A horse and an old army saddle—oh, forty bucks."

"Mister, I ain't got a penny."

"I'll loan it to you."

She chewed her lip, looking doubtful. "No funny business?"

"No funny business."

"When're we going?"

"When the sun sets."

"Huh?" She looked cross at him like she didn't trust him. "Why then?"

"Apaches don't roam at night."

"Good idea," she said softly.

Temperature hadn't cooled any when the sun fired the western sky ablaze and sunk somewhere farther west, making long shadows stretch out from the towering saguaros. Blake used his felt hat to fan himself as he sat in the rocker on the depot porch. The gold braid thumped on the stiff brim.

"By morning, we'll freeze. I guess this is what hell must be like, thorny plants to impale you along with hot days and freezing nights."

"Ain't no climate I ever been in that is perfect," Slocum said, sitting on the bench behind him.

"Madison's going to get that old man mad at him, fooling with his squaw." Blake gave a head toss toward the two of them in the shadows. Madison kissing on her and squeezing a tit every chance he got.

"He damn sure ain't no gentlemen," Slocum said and rose to stretch. "Don't look for me in the morning."

"You cutting out?"

"Planning to."

"Keep your head down. Them bucks got six cartridges."

"Yeah, two of them are mine."

"They ain't going on the warpath with six bullets for God's sake."

Slocum walked to the front of the porch. He leaned on the crooked post to look at the vast country turned purple by the twilight. The crests of the Chiricahuas were still in the rosy light. He gave the captain a wave and went to the coach. He drew out his saddle and gear. The pack on his shoulder, he looked back. He could see the red glow of the officer's cigar he'd lit for his final treat of the day that had gone all wrong.

Inside the depot jacal, they were lighting lamps. Slocum turned and whistled as he strode up the arroyo, feeling the loose sand under his boot soles.

Out of the shadowy mesquite grove, Billie came running after him. "I'm coming," she called out, as her straw hat bounced on her shoulders, the chin string around her throat.

"You ever have any clothes of your own?" Slocum asked, surveying her oversized garb.

"Naw," she said, shuffling along beside him. "I had six older brothers. I never had no girl clothes. Got the ones they outgrew. Probably wouldn't have worn no girl duds anyhow."

"Fred never buy you anything?"

"He didn't care."

Slocum shifted the saddle on his shoulder a little. Damn things were made to fit horses, not be packed. Still, he would need it when they found some horses.

"I owe you four bits now," she said, gazing up at the stars.

"Big debt."

"Ain't funny. I don't have the means to repay you. I done traded off his broke watch, his knife—Lord, he didn't have any money left. I'd knowed we were that broke I'd made him stop and work somewhere."

"He never said."

"Naw, Fred never talked about much but his pipe dreams. How he was going to do this and that and make thousands of dollars."

"Were they good ideas?" He gave the saddle a boost upon the top of his shoulder. She looked up at him and even in the dim light he could see the impatience written on her face.

"Lord, no. They were scatterbrained as a goose's."

"You ever tell him they were crazy?"

"Naw, Fred wasn't mean to me, so I wasn't mean to him. If he'd only listened—I never asked him to do much."

"It wasn't your fault. Quit feeling guilty about it."

"You mean that, don't you?" she said, wrestling the oversize belt and pants waist up.

"I don't say much I don't mean."

"You ain't easy to figure. But when you shut the Messikin up, I figured you was real."

"Madison?"

"Yeah. He was obscene."

"Obscene's a big word."

"I know what it means. I can read. He was obscene. 'Sides he gave me the shivers."

Soon Slocum could see the lights of the Gunny Sack Mine on the far hillside, which meant they were close to a mile from Crystal Springs. He paused and set down the saddle. "We can wait here till dawn. No one that sells anything is up this time of night."

She folded her arms and looked off at the distant mine's lights. He got on his knees and undid the blanket and ground cloth. For his part, she sure could act stubborn.

"You can have the blanket." He held it up to her.

"I ain't taking your blanket." She stood with her feet apart and didn't turn to look at him.

"Be cold up here in another couple of hours."

"I'll be just fine over there." She pointed to some rocks.

"Stomp the rattlesnakes out of them first." He whipped out the canvas ground cloth, unbuckled his gun belt and then sat down to take off his boots.

"I been a 'thinking."

"You changed your mind, you want the blanket?"

"No. I can sleep with you—with our clothes on—and we both won't freeze."

"You can have the blanket."

"I ain't scared of you." She dropped down beside him and unlaced the brogans.

No socks. He could see her massaging her bare foot. They must ache wearing those oversize men's shoes without socks. He didn't even want to think about treating his own feet like that.

"I'm ready," she said and scooted up the ground cloth to be under the thick blanket with him. They both lay down and she turned on her side away from him. He gave a shrug and settled down beside her.

Later, he half awoke and found her form molded to his back. He shut his eyes and went back to sleep. The sun was coming over the Chiricahuas when he woke and spotted her sitting on her butt putting on her shoes.

"I guess they're up now." She finished and clapped her knees. "Guess we can go find them horses."

He agreed and pulled on his own foot gear. "Maybe some breakfast, too."

"Oh, then I'd owe you another two bits."

"You're getting in debt fast," he said and shook his head getting up.

"If that dumb Fred had only listened—"

He stood and rolled up the blanket. The saddle on his shoulder, he motioned for her to start out. They soon struck a road, and headed for Crystal. Twice the dust was stirred up by fast passing rigs and it engulfed them. Slocum was grateful when the breeze swept it away. Neither outfit offered them a ride, which he considered unfriendly. Soon the jacals and shacks of Crystal began to dot the juniper-clad hillsides. Dogs set up barking at the intruders. The two of them followed the crooked road into the canyon where stores and saloons faced each other in a cluster.

A grizzly swamper in a filthy apron came out of the barroom and tossed a pail of mop water into the street. He paused to look at them, then went back inside without comment.

At the livery, the horses and mules were in open corrals and the shedlike structure was marked "Livery—Hosses Sold and Bout."

"He can't spell," she said. "That ain't bought."

"We don't need to sell one so we ain't affected."

She shook her head as if the matter was hopeless.

The owner came out, pulling at his crotch like he had a bad problem and nodded. "What you two guys need?"

Slocum almost smiled, but cut her off with a frown before she could straighten out his conception of her gender.

"Need a couple of good horses."

The man ran his hand down inside his waistband and really worked over his privates.

"I got 'em. Help yourself." With a head toss toward the corral, he continued working on his "itch" problem.

"We'll go look," Slocum said and directed her toward the corral.

"Whatever he's got I damn sure don't want," she said, under her breath.

Slocum glanced back and then turned toward the animals in the pen. Maybe the man would solve his problem while they were inspecting his horses. She stepped up on the fence and pointed to a short bulldog buckskin.

"What about him?"

"Looks okay from here." He took a lead rope off the post and climbed over. The gelding was well-broke and easy to catch when Slocum held his hand out. Rope in hand, he led the horse over to the fence.

His feet looked all right. No splints or ring bone. He appeared to be seven or eight from his teeth and stepped out good.

"Broke to death," the livery man said, joining them. "Broke to drive, too."

"How much?"

"Fifty."

Slocum shook his head. "Twenty."

"Twenty-five and that's low as I go."

"Throw in one of them army saddles and you've got a deal."

"Damn, mister, you're hard to deal with."

"Hand me a lariat," Slocum said and held out his hand. A big roan horse had caught his eye as the others in the pen moved about excited, trying to avoid capture.

"What happened to your horses?" He climbed on the fence and gave Slocum the rope.

"Apaches stole them," Slocum said and threaded out a loop. Keeping it hidden behind his back, he moved to avoid the others that darted past him and attempted to catch the big blue roan when he went by. Up and overhanded, the rope landed around the horse's neck and Slocum jerked the slack. The roan shut down.

He blew rollers out his nose and looked walleyed at Slocum. Trembling, it waited to settle down until Slocum's hand touched his neck and his low voice reassured him. A five-year-old by his teeth, he looked sound to Slocum.

"How much?"

"Thirty and I ain't going any lower. That's a big stout horse.

Them mustangs are cheap." The man shook his head. "But I can sell the likes of him anytime for that much."

"Guarantee he won't buck and I'll pay you thirty or I get him for twenty if he bucks. I'll take him as is at twenty-five."

The livery man, who was about thirty years old with a week's beard stubble, began rubbing his palm over his mouth. No doubt considering whether the roan would bog his head.

"Geez, kid, your old man is hard to deal with. You think he'll buck?" he asked her.

"That sumbitch's liable to buck." She shook her head like she couldn't believe he'd even asked her a question like that.

He frowned at her, then shrugged and nodded in disgust. "Fifty for both and you got a deal. But if I ain't in business when you come by next time you can say I helped put him under."

Their horses saddled, they led them to a building marked "Cafe," which was located about a half block away.

"What was wrong with that guy?" She frowned, looking back down the street at the livery.

"He had an itch."

"Geez—" She shuttered as if repulsed by him. "I don't want it."

Slocum chuckled and opened the door for her. "I doubt you'll get it."

Inside the cafe, which was full of the smells of cooking bacon, a matronly woman waited on them, taking their order and delivering coffee.

"See any Apaches?" She set the steaming cups down in front of them.

"No, not since yesterday."

"Word's out they're all breaking out of San Carlos and going to Mexico."

"Means they'll sweep by here," Slocum said.

"Yeah, this is on the route." The woman glanced out the front window at the street. "Any minute I keep expecting them heathens to ride right in and raid this place."

"Who broke out?"

"Geronimo and a bunch more."

"Gray Fox?"

"I never heard his name mentioned. He's one of them though, so I may not have heard about all of them. You two are newcomers, ain't you?"

"Yes."

"Well, for your safety, you should have stayed somewhere there ain't bloodthirsty damn Apaches." With a sharp nod, she went after their food.

"She don't like them," Billie said and scooped sugar in her coffee.

"Most folks in the territory hate them. They've killed lots of folks."

Idly, she stirred her cup and nodded. "Guess I should to. They kilt Fred."

"That's up to you."

"You hate them?"

He blew the steam off the surface ready to take a drink. "No, but I don't like the mean ones. This used to be their land, we took it."

"After we eat—"

"Well, well, here they are." Madison came striding into the cafe looking at the two of them. "How's the honeymooners?"

When he swaggered over, Slocum caught him by the vest and jerked him close to his face and hissed, "Shut your damn mouth or I'll cut your tongue out."

"Oh, oh, I was only kidding—" Eyes wide open in shock, he staggered backwards from Slocum's hard shove. "I just—"

But Slocum's fierce scowl shut him up and he went off to sit at the counter.

Billie clapped him on the leg under the table. "Thanks, but watch your back. He's the kind that would stab you when you ain't looking."

Through the vapors steaming off the coffee that distorted his vision, he saw an Indian, balancing a rifle on his leg, ride up in front of the cafe.

2

"Apaches!" the woman screamed and dropped the two plates of food as she came out of the kitchen. The clatter of breaking dishes broke the tension of the moment.

Slocum saw Madison jump to his feet and draw his gun. The ex-scout headed for the door and Slocum realized he needed to stop Madison from doing anything stupid like shooting that Apache on horseback.

"Put that gun down or die!" Slocum said. The .44 was in his fist, cocked and aimed at the ex-scout when he turned. In one long stride, he crossed the room, keeping his gun on Madison. "Drop it slow-like on the table."

"That red nigger out there is going to—"

"He ain't got an ounce of war paint on him; if you'd look, he wants to talk."

"Damn funny, he ain't got no clothes on either." The ex-scout put down his gun.

"You had a brain, you'd be dangerous." Slocum swept Madison's Colt off the table, tucked it in his waist and looked over things he could see from inside. Slocum immediately recognized the Indian as Gray Fox. The Apache sat on his horse in the center of the street and looked around.

"Ho," Slocum called out, holstering his own six-gun.

"Ho. You the majordomo?" Gray Fox asked in Spanish.

"No. What do you want?"

"I want my women and children to come stay here until Geronimo is gone to the Madres."

"Why?' " Slocum folded his arms over his chest. Several of the braver souls were beginning to peek around the corners at the two of them.

"Geronimo wants to kidnap our women and children so our men will join him."

"But we're not the army here." Slocum used his open hands to show him. "Take them to San Carlos."

Gray Fox nodded. "But to get up there I must expose them. It is fifty kilometers to Fort Bowie, as far to Fort Grant or Huachuca."

Slocum nodded slowly. "And two or three day's ride."

"Many would have to walk."

"What's he want?" A big man with a bushy red beard asked, standing on the boardwalk twenty feet away.

"He wants you to protect his women and children from Geronimo."

"Why hellfire, we'd be lucky to protect ourselves."

"You an official here?" Slocum asked.

"Mine boss. Clayton's my name."

"Slocum's mine and this is Gray Fox."

Clayton joined him. "How many women and children has he got?"

Slocum asked him in Spanish.

"Thirty in all."

With a nod to show he understood Fox's numbers, Clayton acted deep in thought, then he nodded his head and spoke to Slocum. "I can send word for some troops to get over here and take them up there."

"That'll take two to three days."

Clayton agreed with a wry scowl of defeat. "By then maybe Geronimo will be in Mexico hightailing for the Madres, huh?"

"With some of Gray Fox's bunch," Slocum added.

"I don't know how folks here would take a whole camp of them in town."

"You have any empty building we could use as a headquarters?"

His eyes closed, Clayton shook his head. "You're getting ahead of me. I don't know if the folks here will accept them."

"Listen, I don't owe that killer Geronimo the time of day. But these folks are starving and afraid to move. They're out of ammo to even hunt—"

"Or to kill us. But that's a helluva lot of people to feed."

"We're talking it over," Slocum said to the chief. His dun stomped his hind foot at a biting fly. Gray Fox checked him and nodded.

"They're caught in the cross fire," Slocum said.

"If we shelter them, we maybe get caught in that same deal."

"Chances are good that Geronimo'll head for Mexico and avoid a confrontation."

"And if he don't?" Clayton raised an eyebrow at him for his reply.

Slocum agreed. "Then we see who wins if push comes to shove."

"You staying for the fireworks?"

"I could. No sense being out there wandering around with Geronimo out there, too."

"There's a good-size house up the canyon. No one lives in it and the small spring and well up there might handle them."

"Apaches don't need much water."

"Still three dozen folks are a lot. Ask him if his men will be on the scout for Geronimo. I don't need any surprises."

Slocum explained to Gray Fox about the house and his people staying close to it and not worrying the town folk to death.

"I understand. I must go to Mexico and escort a small band of my people up here," Gray Fox said in Spanish to Clayton. "We will stand guard when we get back."

"Go get them and come right back."

Gray Fox agreed and then turned his pony to leave.

"Slocum," Clayton said, "I'm hiring you to be the agent until we can get some help or the damn army up here. Job pays ten bucks a day, but you handle it all."

"I wasn't asking for any pay."

"I know, but this still can be iffy. You seem to talk their lingo and get along."

"What about me?" Madison asked, leaning his shoulder against the door frame.

"Who the hell are you?" Clayton asked, frowning at the ex-scout.

"Curly Madison, the best damn scout they ever had at Bowie."

"I don't need a scout."

"You hired him." Madison pointed at Slocum.

"One superintendent in charge is enough."

"Oh, I know how to handle them. What does he know?"

"Gawdamnit, I don't need you."

"You'll regret this day." Madison's face black with anger, he held out his hand for his gun.

Deliberately, Slocum ejected the five bullets into his palm and then handed it back.

"Both of you are fools," Madison said and leaped on his horse. "You will regret today the rest for your lives."

"Listen, you greaser bastard, you ever come around here again even threatening me and I'll feed your ass to the buzzards." Clayton's face was red under his beard; his fist closed on the gun butt at his waist.

Madison rode off in a cloud of dust.

"Where were we?" Clayton asked, looking around at the merchants and curious folks gathering in the street to learn what happened.

"You going to send someone to tell the army?"

"Yeah, let me explain to them what we're doing." Clayton held his arms up. "Listen everyone—"

Slocum saw Billie, fighting her sleeves, standing in front of their horses.

"What now?" she asked.

"We're going to run the Injun camp for a few days."

"We're *what*?" She narrowed her eyes in a pained expression.

"Easy," he said, looking back to see if anyone heard her. "It's only until the army gets here to take them to San Carlos."

"Geez, Slocum, they might shoot us like they did Fred."

He shook his head. "They only want some help."

"Where'll we stay?" She looked bewildered.

"We'll find us a place. Clayton's about through telling them the deal."

Clayton came over to them. "There's a building belongs to the mine up the end of that street, got some housekeeping stuff in it. You and the boy can stay there. Pen for the horses, too."

"What's it look like?" Slocum asked.

"Last one at the head of the canyon. You can't miss it."

"I'll keep an eye out. You be at the mine?"

"Yeah, give me some reports on what you need. I'll send some food and stuff."

"I'll let you know how it goes." Slocum took the reins and checked the girth. "We'll go check out the place."

"See you," Clayton said and stomped off down the wooden boardwalk in his knee-high, lace-up boots.

"He's just giving you a job and house?" she asked, climbing on her buckskin.

"He needed someone to handle it."

"Sure, but he didn't know you from Adam's off ox."

"He didn't hire Madison, did he?"

"No, and he sure run him off, too. I was glad. I think he's a big troublemaker."

Slocum agreed and mounted his horse. His full attention centered on the roan as he checked him. Bowed up underneath him, the roan sure seemed like he might buck. The horse danced around as Slocum tried to stop him. Billie giggled.

"It ain't funny."

"You really could've bought him cheaper."

At the edge of the business district, Slocum sent the roan up the wagon tracks that Clayton called a street. In a long trot to take some of the steam out of him, Slocum fought the roan's desire to bog his head. Billie came on a short lope after him.

The building was weathered gray clapboard on the outside and stuffy inside. Billie went to opening doors and the few window to air it out. Slocum put the horses in the pen, loosened their cinches and let them eat the old hay in the bunker.

When he came back, she had a broom and was sweeping the floor.

"Found two damn scorpions so far," she said and he nodded.

Better go to dumping his boots or he might find one in them. He was grateful the place would be out of sight of the townspeople. It might be easier having Apaches in their backyard if they couldn't see them.

"When're them Apaches coming?" She stopped and leaned on the handle.

"Damned if I know. There's a tank of water out there will do fine to bathe in. I'm going to have me a bath."

"Won't hurt either of us."

"You first?"

She looked at him and sucked on her side teeth. "I don't reckon I've got anything you ain't seen before or won't see after that."

"Your call."

"I've got two feed sack towels and you've got a bar of soap in your gear."

"Let's hit the water."

"Fine with me."

A small stream of water coming from a rusty pipe spilled into a stone tank. She stopped beside it and sat on the ground taking off her brogans. Slocum toed off his boots and then removed his socks.

She undid the too-big belt buckle and the pants fell to her ankles. Her snowy white legs flashed shapely in the morning sunlight. Tiny fingers fumbled through the buttons on the shirt and soon she shed it.

He looked over at her mildly as she hugged her small proud breasts with folded arms. "Bet the water's cold."

She laughed uneasy, chewing on her lip and shuffling her bare feet, as she stared at the water tank. "I'm shivering thinking about it."

"It ain't heated, that's for sure."

"Best way is to jump in." She wrinkled her nose. "Could you lift me up and over?"

"Sure, in a minute." He shed his pants and then his underwear.

"That damn Fred lied to me." Her blue eyes narrowed in anger.

"About what?" He swept her up in one swift motion.

She grasped his face on both sides and kissed him hard on the mouth. Then she broke loose and smiled at him, highlights danced in her eyes. "About him having the biggest dick in the world."

"Did he?"

"Hell, no, and I know the truth now."

She shrieked when he swept her up and dropped her in the water. Then she struck out swimming across the tank. Her sleek, shapely body was like an otter's in the water.

"You can sure swim," he said, easing himself over the side.

"I was raised in Arkansas. My brothers taught me how to swim when I was little."

"You must have been real small then."

"Quit picking on me." Billie sliced off a wave at him.

"I'll do that," he said, lathering up and handing her the soap.

"I been thinking—guess you could tell."

"What's that?"

"Fred's gone. Ain't no need in saving it no longer is there?"

"What's that?" He tried to suppress his grin.

"Damn you, Slocum, you've knowed all the time what I'm talking about."

"Oh, that—" He paused and frowned to silence her. In three long steps through the water, he was at his holster and held the gun in his hand.

She whirled around to see what it was and then turned back. "We ain't alone?"

Slocum listened. "Either a cat or a coati." He put the Colt back in the holster. "Where were we?"

"Oh, damn you. I'm clean now—what are you doing?"

"Going to carry you to the house," he said, sweeping her up in his arms.

"Get your gun and the towels on our way."

"Good idea." With no effort, he sat on the wall with her in his arms, dripping water all over. He swiveled around for her to get the two items, then he headed for the house.

Inside, she put the holster on the table and he let her down. With a towel, she began to dry his chest, working lower and lower until she dried off his privates and stared at the half stiff rod. "He must get even bigger."

Then she looked up at him with a sly grin. "I can't wait."

She led him to the iron poster bed and in seconds was standing on it, arms encircled around his neck. Her rock hard nipples nailed into his chest and her hot mouth and tongue consumed his. His hands ran over her tight ass and cupped the half moons. When he felt her left breast, she sucked in her breath. When he tasted the right one, she clutched his head to her and stifled a scream.

"Oh, geez, Slocum take me—now."

While he scrambled to get on the bed, she dropped to her butt, spread her short legs apart and held up her arms for him. He used his right hand for a guide and slid the nose of his erection in the gates. With both of her hands, she raised her butt for him.

Slow-like, he began to probe his dick around her tight center. She threw her head back and when he looked down he could see the strained cords of her neck as she cried out. "Oh, geez, Slocum, I love it."

She laid open her legs for him, until he was grinding on her pubic bone. His swollen erection was on fire as he pumped into her. Both of them were breathing like runaway horses with the world whirling by them. She clung to him and came.

Her blue eyes looked glazed over when he drove his rod home hard and deep, exploding deep inside of her. Billie's lashes closed and her mouth fell open. Slocum bent down and kissed her limp lips; she had fainted!

"You all right?" he asked, concerned.

Billie raised up on her elbows and shook her head to clear it. "I was married for a year and a half and I never ever fainted after doing it. And we must have done it once a day, sometimes more—whew, that was wonderful."

"Nice," he said, on his knees between her legs.

"I know that look." She blinded at him in disbelief. "You want to do it again?"

"No, I want you to faint again."

Billie held up her arms for Slocum to come back on top of her.

3

"Where're they coming from?" Billie asked with frown. "They come in like smoke."

Slocum nodded. Apache women and children had begun to show up at the large house that once may have housed a school. Inside, Slocum had found some paper and pencils in a cupboard. Outside, they'd found a well. The bucket was on a chain and he'd drawn several pails up to fill a trough and tasted it. Not bad. It didn't have some dead animal floating in its shadowy depth. They'd be all right.

With the paper and pencil, he'd made a list of things he'd need. Lights were on the top of it. Two burly men from the mine had left him two hundred-pound sacks of pinto beans, some salt and some rancid-looking bacon that Billie had turned her nose up at. A big cooking kettle, a large coffeepot and no coffee beans. His count of the women was six, so far, and eight children ages baby to ten. But more were streaming in.

The Apache women squatted in the shade of the cottonwoods as if waiting.

"I'd better send them after some firewood," Slocum said and Billie agreed. He also wrote axes on his list. "Those beans will take some time to cook."

"Who's the boss?" he asked them in Spanish and they giggled.

"We need to build a fire and cook my beans." He rubbed his stomach. "For your bellies, too. Better gather some firewood for cooking."

A community nod went around and they got up and began to

31

drag in wood. He broke up some small stuff. Billie found him a handful of bunch grass and soon he struck a match. Flames licked up through the yellow stems into the small branches. Slocum continued to break up what he could to put on it.

Billie gave a scream and Slocum turned in time to see a squaw holding an ax.

"You need this," she said in English.

"Yes, what is your name?" he asked and stepped over to take it.

"Mary Jones." The short woman was hard-eyed, despite her generous offer. The dark skin on her face was drawn tight as a drum top, and it was obvious from her thin shoulders that she had been on subsistence rations.

"My name's Slocum. That is Billie."

She never released the ax. "I can use it. This is women's work."

He stepped back. "Whatever you say. Billie, go up to the store and get us a chunk of good bacon on our account and some coffee."

"We got an account?" She closed her right eye and looked hard at him.

"Charge it to Clayton."

"Coffee, too?"

"Yes and some sugar."

Mary Jones spoke to some of the women who were holding back and they joined her. Two of them went to the beans and began to unthread the top of the first sack. The kettle was put on the fire and another squaw went for water. The first pail was dumped in and grins soon covered their looks of anticipation. They made the fire hotter and chopped up the pieces too large to break. Their efforts soon had a crackling fire under the pot.

The brown-skinned children all sat in the shade, quietly speaking in whispers to each other. Most wore only short shirts, so despite their dusty condition it was obvious who was a boy and who was a girl. One woman seated on the ground breastfed a baby. Slocum doubted she had much milk in her flat breasts. The whole bunch looked malnourished. The hip bones on the children stuck out.

Slocum watched the women sort the beans, then take pans full of the picked ones to dump into the pot. Mary Jones came over. "How long must this last us?"

"When we need more I will go get some. I sent Billie after some better bacon. Don't use that."

"We have had worse."

"Wait, she will bring us coffee, too."

"As you say—patron."

"I am not the patron. I am the amigo."

She shook her head. "We have had little food in many days. This is the feast of a patron."

"I see her coming. Better heat some water in the big coffeepot."

A genuine smile crossed her thin lips and she nodded. "I have not had coffee in many moons."

"Do you have cups enough for all?"

"Why?"

"She has sugar, too. The children will want some."

Billie jumped off her buckskin and ran over. "You better go up to town. I heard them say they were getting armed to kill this bunch."

"No, they mean in case that Geronimo comes."

"No, they meant to kill these women and children."

"Madison behind this?"

"I never saw him."

Mary and the other women carried the supplies from Billie's horse up to the porch.

"The coffee beans've been roasted," Billie said to Mary.

"Good. We can grind them."

When she was gone, Slocum turned back to Billie. "You sure I've got troubles?"

"Clayton was nowhere around and they were all going into the cantina."

"Getting fortified to come up here, no doubt." Slocum shook his head. No one said this job would be easy. He might sure earn his "easy money."

"What'll we do?" Billie half-whispered.

"I better go see how serious it is."

"Want me to stay here?"

"Yes. Keep an eye on things. I won't be gone long."

"You be careful; they sounded mad."

"I will. Mary will do what you ask her to do."

Stretching her arms out and pushing her sleeves back, she nodded. "Oh, I'll be fine."

Slocum drew up the cinch on the roan, swung a leg over and

headed into town. He passed the store and saw the load of horses tied at the hitch rack in front of the saloon. Slocum dismounted a short distance from the saloon, hitched the roan and walked over to the cantina.

"Boys, we got us a rat's nest out there at the old hall. Bunch of them Apaches are gathering up to rape our women and steal our livestock." He waited for the crowd to urge him on.

"What do we need to do, Leo?"

"We need to go out there and kill every mother son of them."

"Yeah," went up the chorus. Beer was sloshed out of schooners and men got on their feet to cheer him on.

"What's for you, stranger?" asked the barkeep, a short guy with straight black hair.

"Beer's fine. What's the ruckus about?"

"Apaches, got a couple hundred up in the canyon. Bad deal."

Slocum nodded that he'd heard him. Then he turned, hooked his elbows on the bar and studied Leo's back as he went on about the Apaches.

"That damn Clayton's brought them in here to run off all the white guys from working at the mine so he can bring in some cheap labor."

"I never trusted that bastard," one well-oiled guy shouted from the front table. "He's a damn company man and he wants them slant-eyed, wormy bastards in that hole. Hell, they'll work for rice."

"Yeah."

"I say that we go up there and kill every one of them Apache killers and all their spawn."

"Who'll be the first to die?" Slocum asked in a soft voice.

"What—" Leo whirled and looked out of his deep blue eyes hard at Slocum as he raised the beer to sip it.

"You going to stop us?"

"Never said that. But you attack them Apaches they'll kill a few of you. Any man in here ready to die?"

"What do you say we should do?" some heckler shouted.

"They sent for the army to take this bunch to San Carlos. The real enemy out there is Geronimo. He's probably raiding your places right now—seeing that you ain't there to guard it."

"Thought he went to Mexico."

Slocum shook his head. "He's back here looking for horses and captives. Probably raiding your places right now."

"How do you know so much?"

Slocum considered the foam on the beer, then looked up. "Trust me. He's out there."

"What in the hell's your business here?" Leo demanded as several men rushed for the door.

"Passing through."

"I'd've had all them sumsbitches dead in an hour."

Slocum nodded. "You might have."

"Listen, you Injun-loving sumbitch—" Leo made a round-house swing at Slocum, who threw up his left arm to ward off the blow. Then he delivered a right to Leo's jaw that set him on his ass.

Rubbing his chin, Leo looked up from the filthy floor and sputtered, "I ought to—"

"You touch that gun butt and you better have a casket picked out, mister."

"What's your name?"

"Slocum. You can find me out at that hall until the army gets here."

"I come out there you'll damn sure need a cemetery plot."

"Don't overload your ass." He turned back to the bartender. "What do I owe you?"

The man dismissed his concern. "It was paid for."

Slocum nodded and headed for the door. Only a few drunks were left. There'd be no backup for the man. But he'd need to talk to Clayton. This Leo had a thorn in his butt about more than Apaches.

"Anything happen in town?" Billie asked, jerking up her pants by the great belt buckle so she could come over to him.

"Oh, there was crowd at the saloon wanting to come out and kill all these bloodthirsty Apaches."

Her eyes flew open. "They coming?"

"No, I sent them home to watch out for Geronimo."

"He around here?" She whirled around to look for him.

"Gray Fox thinks he'll come back for these women and children."

"Geez, we're between a rock and a hard place, ain't we?"

"Somewhere like that." He stripped off his saddle and paused with it in his hands to look at her. "I was going to buy some material and get a dress made for you."

She wrinkled her nose at him. "I don't need no dress."

"Yes, you do. You'd be cute in a dress and no one can tell you from a boy in that oversize rig."

"Aw, Slocum." Her face turned red. "I'd never make no woman."

"Yes, you would and I'm going to find you an outfit to wear that fits you. Clayton been by?"

"No, but more women and children are coming in. And they're all hungry. Don't guess they've had much to eat."

"Wagon's coming," he said, seeing the dust and hearing the drum of hooves.

"I don't think they've had enough to eat for long time," she said walking beside him to go out and greet the rig.

"You're probably right. Wonder who this is?"

The man on the seat reined in the team and jerked the brake on. "You must be Slocum." he shouted and bailed off the rig.

"Never caught yours?" He shook the man's calloused paw.

"Vi's mine. Clayton said you'd need more supplies. I've got a front quarter of beef, tarped down. Two fat sheep, I butchered this morning, and some flour, lard, coffee and sugar."

"I'll go get Mary Jones," Billie said and took off, gathering her clothes as she went.

"That your boy?" Vi asked.

"Actually she's a young woman. Apaches killed her husband, took all she had and she's kind of been abandoned."

"Could have fooled me."

"Her oversized clothes have protected her I think."

"Yeah, bet they have."

"You have a butcher shop?"

"Sure do and I appreciate the business."

"Not near as much as these Apaches will the meat."

"They starving?"

Slocum nodded as Billie led the Mary Jones and five other squaws toward the wagon.

Vi climbed up and threw back the tarp. "Fresh beef," he said and hoisted the front quarter up to the side.

Mary sent two of the women for it. Then her eyes grew larger at the sight of the first sheep carcass. "Is there more?"

"One more sheep."

"Oh." She began to call out in Apache, waving for help. They came on the run, flashes of bare brown legs showing from under pleated skirts to help her. Mary turned and looked for Slocum.

"Did you do this?"

"No, the man at the mine sent all this."

"Why does he do this?"

Slocum thought for minute before he spoke. "Guess he wants you fed well while you are his guests."

She looked toward the piles of rock waste and the entrance high on the mountain. "Maybe we can thank him in some way."

"Oh, I'm sure that you can."

Vi was off the wagon and he nodded to her. "How long will that last?"

"Oh, my, so much—they will eat that today."

"I'll bring out some more tomorrow."

"Gracias," she said and smiled.

"See you then," Vi said and climbed on his wagon.

"Yes," Mary said and turned back to Slocum. "Come and eat with us. The frijoles are wonderful."

He'd need for Gray Fox to set up some guards whenever he arrived. No telling where he and the bucks were but he wished they'd get there—before someone stupid like Leo tried an attack.

4

"Who's that?" Billie asked, looking at the boiling dust coming up the canyon.

Seated on a bench under the porch, Slocum looked up from his plate of brown beans and tried to make out the driver who slammed the horses to a halt and then looked over the camp of wide-eyed children and squaws. He wore a derby hat, a brown suit and tie.

"You must be Slocum," he said and made a straight line for him. "I'm the mayor of Crystal Springs and I was over in Tombstone while all this was going on. My heavens, aren't you afraid, you and the boy here, of being scalped?"

"Billie and I ain't worried about Apaches. We're more worried about Leo inciting a mob to come up here and hurt lots of folks." He shared a private don't-bother look with her.

"I heard about you backing him down. He's trouble all the time. I don't know why he don't move on. Used to freight for the mine, but got drunk one too many times on the job and Clayton fired him."

"That explains that part. What do you need?"

"Tom Jackson. I was worried you needed help."

"Tom, I just need a handle on the troublemakers from town until the army arrives."

The man agreed and looked puzzled at the camp. "Where did they get all this food they're cooking?"

"Clayton sent it."

"They were starving," Billie said.

"My, my, I never thought about them starving."

"They were," Billie assured him.

"Well, I'll do all I can about the mob business, if I have to jail Leo Krier."

"Thanks. All these folks want is to be left alone."

"Good to meet you two." He tipped his hat to them.

Slocum agreed and watched the man step onto the buggy, undo the reins and leave in a cloud of dust.

"What next?" Billie asked, checking the sun time.

"We just wait for Gray Fox to come back."

"Where did he go?"

"Maybe Mary knows. But he's going to miss some good food later on if he don't get back."

"You serious about me and a dress?"

"Serious as I can be."

She scuffed the toe of the brogan in the dust. "I ain't never been a girl."

"You're a helluva girl."

"Geez, Slocum, you make it sound easy."

"Hide out if you want to in them clothes, but I know the difference."

She took his empty plate and shook her head. "You're just easy pleased."

"No," he said, studying the hillside above their camp that glinted like diamonds where the afternoon sun shone on the specs of mica. "You're a neat woman in a small package."

"When're you going to see Clayton?" she asked to change the subject.

"Better do it before sundown. The man he sent should be at one of the forts by now."

"That mean the army should be here tomorrow?"

"You don't know about the military. They may be out on patrol and have no one to send. They may have to wire Washington for permission and wait on a reply. There are all kinds for things to keep them from coming right over here."

"But I thought—"

"You thought that the army wanted to solve the Apache problem?" He shook his head. "For them and the Tucson Ring, it's the only war they've got."

She wrinkled her nose at him. "Tucson Ring?"

"There's a big ring of businessmen in Tucson that live off the profits of providing the needs of the U.S. army and they don't want that to stop."

"What will they try to do?"

"Get the Apaches drunk. Sell them arms. They have no conscience. Just so the Apache war continues."

"Who are they?"

"A man named Ferrell Stone is the biggest one."

"He lives in Tucson?"

"Yes."

"And the law won't do anything about it?"

"No, they're all big business people."

"Bunch of crap. Geez."

"It always has been. Mary's coming." He rose to his feet from the bench. "Something wrong?"

"No, tonight we will feast and want you both to come join us."

"We'd come, but Billie don't have a dress."

"Oh, we can fix that," she said and took Billie by the arm.

"Geez, Slocum, damn you, I don't need a dress."

He nodded that she did and Mary swept her away.

"I'll go see Clayton, while you get a dress," he said after her. Then he laughed at his trick—maybe he'd get to enjoy watching her as a woman when he got back.

An hour later, Slocum found Clayton at the mine office.

"How's it going?" the mine boss asked.

"Good, so far. Must have over thirty women and children in camp. The men were still out when I left."

"The men'll come in, won't they?"

"I expect they're hunting."

"But I sent meat and supplies."

"Yes, and very generous of you. But the men don't know about that yet."

"Of course. I'm anxious to hear from my man I sent to Fort Bowie."

"He should be back tomorrow," Slocum said.

"Right, maybe tonight."

"You know the military can act fast or slow."

"I expect slow, but they should be here in a week and take these folks up there. I also heard about you taking on Krier. Sorry."

"He's no problem unless he raises a mob."

"I should have run him off when I fired him."

"We all have done the same thing with his kind—never really finished with them. I'll get back to the camp."

"I appreciate you doing this. I don't know where you came from or your business, but thanks. I think we'll all be better off if these Apaches are up there on the San Carlos reservation and not in Mexico helping Geronimo make more mischief."

Slocum agreed and stood.

"Vi told me you'd need more meat."

"They're hungry."

"I'll have him bring meat and more beans."

"We have enough of the rest."

Clayton rose, stuck out his hand. "Order what you'll need the next day from him."

"I'll handle it."

"I'm not concerned," Clayton said and showed him out. "Need anything, let me know."

Slocum stepped in the stirrup, saluted the big man and set off down the mountain. He took the side trail that wound off through the junipers and made his way into the side canyon on the trail.

He wasn't expecting the pony and rider that rushed out of a small thicket in the bushy evergreens at the last minute. The hard-eyed buck held out a lever-action Winchester. The roan shied and Slocum reached for his Colt, trying to control the spooked horse. The shrill screams coming from behind the Apache's barred teeth made him fearsome.

Smoke mushroomed out the muzzle of the rifle. He missed. The .44 barked in Slocum's hand and the bullet took the small rider in the chest, spilling him off the shying horse.

Slocum whirled the roan around looking for the next Apache to come screaming down on him. Seeing nothing, he dropped to the ground, reins in one hand, and the still-smoking gun in the other. His heart pounded hard under his breastbone as he stepped over some prickly pear cactus. Filled with anxiety, he went to where the Apache lay on the ground. Using his boot, he turned him over. The dark eyes stared for eternity at the azure sky.

Apaches hated the dead. But he needed to know who this buck belonged to. Was he one of Geronimo's renegades or a stray bronco? There were plenty of them along the Mexican border;

they owed no one allegiance and survived making small attacks on the unsuspecting.

Slocum holstered the Colt, loaded the limp body over his saddle and picked up the Winchester. He paused for a moment to remove his spurs and hang them on the horn; they could tangle him up going down the steep trail on foot. Then he set out for the camp.

Coming down the valley under a few gnarled cottonwoods, he blinked at the girl coming to greet him. In a pleated skirt that hugged her trim waist, she ran up the brown grass in white squaw boots.

"What happened?"

"He wanted my gun and horse." With a head toss toward the corpse, he smiled looking at the fresh young woman, nodding in approval.

"Feels funny not to have pants on," Billie said and hugged his arm.

"Looks nice."

"I'm only doing it for you. What about him?"

"I hope Mary or one of the women can tell me who he is."

"Pretty brazen, huh? I mean you weren't far from camp. I heard the shots."

"Let's see who the buck is." He headed for the campfires.

Mary came to meet him and looked apprehensive at the dead man.

"Who is he?"

She never went closer and shook her head. "Maybe Lupe will know." She waved a shorter women over.

Lupe carried a long healed scar across her cheek and she went to the dead buck, grabbed a fistful of his hair and raised his head up to look at him.

"He's the one called Many Lives," she said in Spanish.

Slocum walked over and asked her, "Is he one of Geronimo's men?"

"He sometimes rides with him. But he is also a loner. He once dragged my sister in the bushes and raped her when we were camped on the San Pedro. It is good he is dead."

"But he's a bronco, too."

Lupe nodded.

"What does that mean?" Billie asked, as the bright glow of sundown cast a red-gold color over the camp.

"We don't know if Geronimo's out there or not." He wished he knew how close the renegade leader was to them.

"They wait for you to come eat with them," Billie said, guiding him to the camp.

"We will see he is put away," Mary said and she took the reins of the roan. "Go eat."

"He can wait. Join us."

Mary smiled. "Men should eat first, then the women and children."

"We are one in my camp."

"I will come as you are the patron."

"I am only a friend."

Mary laughed. "No, only a patron could get us all this food."

Seated on a blanket, he was at the head of a double row of women and children. In the growing twilight, he watched the hungry children gnaw at rib bones to secure every string of meat. Their smiles warmed him as he ate.

Billie sat cross-legged in her new outfit beside him. "Will the army come soon for them?"

"You going to miss them?"

"They have been very nice to me."

"One of them killed your husband."

She shook head. "No, not any of them or even that renegade you brought in."

"He will show up."

"I won't forget him."

"Mary, we need some women to stand guard tonight. Between Geronimo and this Krier, I don't want to be taken by surprise."

"I will assign them. No one will get into camp."

"Good. Don't sleep in this open area. Go up on the hills in case they try."

"You think they will try?" Mary asked.

"I think we must be careful. We have few weapons amongst us."

"What can I do?" Billie asked.

"Be ready for anything. And wake me up before the sun rises." He laughed and selected another beef rib from his plate. "I don't want to be sleeping if they try."

"Lupe can shoot a rifle," Mary said. "She's better than most men."

"Good, give her the one I took from the dead one. Tell her to be sure who she shoots. Not our friends."

Mary smiled. "I will."

The meal over, Slocum took Billie and their bedding uphill from the hall. In the starlight he could see the women and children fading into the junipers over on the slopes.

If someone charged into camp they wouldn't find anyone. This might also give the women and children a chance to vanish into the countryside. Guards out, he felt they were ready in the case of an attack. But he wished the men would come back. Thirty women and children was a lot of responsibility.

He slipped off his gun belt, dropped it on the bedding, he had spread out in a place he'd cleared of rocks with his boot. Billie stood with her arms folded, waiting until he stepped over in front of her.

"You make a lovely woman," he said and turned up her chin with the side of his hand. Her eyes were closed tight and she didn't answer. "You all right?"

"Hold me tight. I'm shaking inside. I know why I never wore women's clothing. I feel so insecure in them."

His arms hugged her and then he lifted her up to kiss her mouth. The anxiousness became hungry passion as her hot tongue sought his. He savored her eagerness and gently laid her on the blanket and let himself down beside her. His right hand molded her firm breast and their breath raged out their nostrils like racing horses.

Soon his hand was beneath the cloth of the blouse and she arched her back to his touch as he teased the rock-hard nipple and then raised the hem with both hands to feast on them. The low moan in her throat came forth as he suckled on the right one, then the left and his palm went over her pubic mound under the skirt.

"Oh, let me undress," she cried in a whisper.

He raised up and stripped his shirt over his head, then rose to toe off his boots and remove his pants. Under him in the starlight, she arranged her snowy body on her back and held up her arms to invite him to join her. Already his stiff dick throbbed in pained turgidity to probe her as he kneeled between her open legs, moving to lower himself on top.

Her small fingers grasped his shaft and guided him in her wet gates. She stiffened for a second as the head passed through her tight ring. When he began to probe in and out of her, she raised her tight ass off the blanket to meet him and the walls of her cunt tightened with each stroke. He fought the battle of finding the treasure deep inside her. The world swirled in his brain, his hips ached with the urge to explode. The head of his inflated dick was close to blowing up. Pubic bone to pubic bone they ground out their wildest needs to be one.

Then from deep in his scrotum, his testicles were squeezed hard in the grasp of an invisible hand. The hot volcanic eruption flew up the tubes and and like a giant water spout he filled her full of his hot cum. She gripped his arms in a finger-tight grasp, then she collapsed underneath him.

He bent over and kissed her soft lips. Waited for her revival. When she didn't come to, he looked hard in the silver light at her.

"Billie?" he whispered.

"Oh, let me sleep," she moaned at last. "With him inside me."

"Be kind of hard."

"It's hard to give him up." She slurred like a drunk.

"I'll be here."

When he was lying beside her, she threw an arm over him. "Forever?"

"No, one day I must leave."

"Why?"

"Oh, men will come looking for me. Men that would harm you, too."

"I don't want you to leave me."

He hugged her tight. "I don't either, but there is no other way."

"Where will you go?"

"Where the wind takes tumbleweeds. I don't know."

"Geez, Slocum, I'll cry and hate being a woman all over again."

"You can cross that river when you come to it."

She rolled over and squirmed on her back. "When Fred made love I liked it. But geez, I never got this excited. I can't believe I did that."

Slocum was on his knees, holding his six-gun in one swift move.

"What is it?" she hissed.

He shook his head to silence her and peered into the night. Something was amiss—

5

A burst of pistol shots cut the night. Broken glass tinkled from the hall's shattered windows. Riders were charging up and down the flat, shooting at any and everything. Slocum pressed Billie down and, seated on his butt, pulled on his pants. Then his boots.

"Who are they?"

"White men, I imagine. Stay low." He was up and gone. More than anything he wanted one of them to interrogate, so he could learn who was the leader.

"Sumbitch, they ain't here!" someone cussed out in front when Slocum made the back of the building. The six-gun in his hand, he edged himself for the corner.

"Wiley's right, there ain't no Injuns here."

"The sumbitch tricked us."

Slocum moved down the side and reached the corner. His gun was cocked and ready. "Hands high or die."

"It's a trap!"

Six-guns belched red-orange flames, others struck on empty. His first shot was at the figure standing on the porch who had been talking. He screamed he was hit; then Slocum shot at the outline on the horse. That one dropped his pistol on the ground. His panicked horse spun out from beneath him and spilled him on the ground. The rest of the gang raced out of camp.

The one on the porch was crying how he was dying. The other raider on the ground had not moved, but Slocum thought he might not be playing possum.

"You all right?" Billie asked.

46

"Fine. Find a candle lamp," he said, easing himself across the porch and making certain in the half light that the wounded one had no gun.

"Everyone is all right over here," Mary called out to Slocum.

"Good, I have two of them."

Billie lit the lamp and carried it out of the hall.

"Who're you?" he asked the blanch-faced cowboy.

"Thurman Yost." He was holding his wounded arm.

"Who's your dead friend?"

"Kell Mitchell."

"Guess Leo got away?"

Yost never answered. Filled with anger, Slocum grasped the cowboy by his vest and jerked him off the ground. "Answer me. Was Leo Krier here tonight?"

"Yeah, yeah."

"He lead this bunch."

"Yeah."

Slocum let him slip to the ground and drew in a deep breath. He closed his eyes. He'd handle Krier in the morning.

"Get his gun and holster," he said and the closest squaw shoved him down and went to unbuckling it while Yost cried she was going to kill him.

Mary sent another to take the dead man's outfit. "Lupe decided they couldn't get anyone, so she didn't shoot."

"Tell her fine. I don't want anyone killed we don't have to."

"What about me?" Yost asked.

"You won't die." His mind rushed with ideas about what he must do next.

"What're you going to do with me?"

"After them squaws castrate you with a dull, rusty knife, I'll take you to town for the law to put you away."

"No!" Yost howled.

"Just sit there and think about it. You came to rape and kill them."

"How will you haul them to town?" Billie asked, setting down the candle lamp

"Vi can haul them back on his meat wagon," he said. "I'm going to town and find Krier."

"I'm going, too. You'll need someone to hold the horses," she said.

In thirty minutes, he left Mary in charge of the prisoner, with orders not to torture him. Billie and Slocum rode under the stars for Crystal Springs. Slocum wondered about many things. Why had Gray Fox and his men not returned? How long could he hold the mob off the Apaches and how long would the army be getting there? All things that bore heavy on his conscience as they trotted toward town.

"Where does this Krier live?"

"Someone will know."

"You're very upset," she said, riding beside him.

"Busy thinking. I'm not upset about you."

"Good, I would rather be in your blanket than in this saddle."

He laughed aloud, then reached out and gave her a shake. "I kinda figured you didn't like doing that."

"That's all changed." She shook her head at him.

A Shanghai rooster greeted them riding up the main street. Perched on the rail corral of the livery, he shook his wattles, threw his head back and really crowed when they rode past. Lights were on in a cafe and Slocum gave a head toss in that direction. They dropped out of the saddle. He checked the loads in his Colt and motioned for her to go behind him.

At the window, he could see Vi in there eating. The other faces were not familiar so he nodded his approval and entered the cafe with her behind him.

Vi looked up and let out a soft whistle. "I thought—"

Slocum gave a head shake to silence him and looked over the others who acted disinterested in the two. Then they joined Vi at his table.

"What's wrong?" The butcher frowned and nodded warmly at Billie.

"They shot up the camp last night," Slocum said.

"Hit anyone?"

"No, but one of them is dead and one wounded. You'll need to bring them in when you deliver the meat this morning."

Vi nodded toward Billie. "Who's she?" A smile swept over his face and his eyes twinkled looking at Billie.

"Billie Barton is her name. Apaches killed her husband and they took all she had. I met her up at the stage station."

"Mrs. Barton, I'm sure pleased to meet'cha."

Vi's words made her blush and she tried to hide by looking at the onc-page menu.

"Where does Krier live?" Slocum asked, but had to stop to give their order for breakfast to the waitress.

"He's got a place up Dry Fork Wash."

"Far away?"

"No, a couple of miles. You going up there and settle with him?"

"Won't be no peace until I do."

Vi held his coffee cup up ready to sip it. "You want help?"

Slocum shook his head. "But thanks."

"I guess I'd better get up to your camp. I've got half a beef for you. That be enough?"

"For today, yes. I'm looking for Gray Fox to come in. But that much meat'll do."

"They ain't big cattle I'm getting, but they're fat, so I figured that much would be enough."

"It tasted good last night," Billie added.

"So you're pleased?" he asked, looking hard at her.

She glanced away as if uncomfortable over the attention. "Better ask the patron. Slocum's the one in charge."

"It was very good beef," Slocum said, over his steaming cup of coffee. "Tell me how to get to Dry Fork Wash."

"Take the main road north, first major dry wash, turn left. The road runs right up the wash. It's about a half mile west. There's a grove of cottonwoods at his place. First ones you'll see going up."

"Who'll be there?" Slocum asked.

"He's got some riffraff hangs around him."

"Texas toughs?"

"Texas cowboys—you know who I mean."

"Good enough. I'll tell Mayor Jackson that you're bringing in a prisoner and he can turn him over to the sheriff."

After the meal, Slocum and Billie rode over to the mayor's furniture and undertaking business. Slocum dismounted, gave her the reins and went inside. He found the man in an apron busy carpentering a casket.

"Make one more for the mob member that got killed last night," Slocum said.

"Who was he?"

"Ken Mitchell."

Jackson put down his hammer. "Sorry I didn't get word that they were on the prowl."

"No matter, we handled it. I've also got Thurman Yost. He's wounded and he says that Krier was leading the deal. Vi's bringing him in. Send him over to the sheriff in Tombstone and charge him with all you can."

"Yes, that might scare any more from trying something. Damn. I'm sorry."

"I'm headed for Krier's. I intend to call him out and settle this."

"Watch he don't shoot you in the back."

"I will, if you can handle the rest."

"I can and will."

Slocum left the man who'd followed him to the door. Jackson nodded at Billie and they rode off.

"I don't know if I like how men look at me in this outfit," she said when they trotted past the last shack in town.

"Flattery," Slocum said. "Pure flattery."

"Yeah and they all are looking like they want to undress me."

"They only want to do that because you are a good-looking woman."

Her face turned red with embarrassment, and she chewed on her lower lip. "Aw, damn you, Slocum."

"You know Fred knew that."

"Huh?" She bolted upright in the saddle. "What did he know?"

"He knew as long as you dressed like an orphan no one would steal you from him."

"I'll be gone to hell." She slapped her forehead with her palm and then shook her head. "You know, I bet you're right."

"This must be the road to his place—" He reined up the roan and looked over the wide sandy bed of the dry wash. Wagon and horse tracks dotted the soft ground. He gave a head toss and they went west.

"We get up here, you stay back. There's liable to be shooting."

"You ain't afraid?" She looked upset at him.

"No, why?"

"My guts been rolling round since we left Crystal."

"There's a good chance he ain't even here. If he thinks Yost told on him, maybe he's hiding."

She nodded half-heartedly. "I'm still nervous."

A dog started barking long before they reached sight of the place under the green cottonwoods. Some corrals and a jacal. A woman was in the yard hanging wash and she looked hard at their approach.

"Stay here," he said and booted the roan on.

In a wash-worn dress, the thin woman, in her late twenties, swept the wave of dark hair from her face and looked up at him.

"Krier here?"

She shook her head. "Ain't seen him in a day. What do you need?"

"To see him."

"I sure don't know when he'll be back. He owes you money, I sure ain't got any to pay you."

Slocum shook his head. "No, idea where he is?"

"Mister, if I did, I'd go find him myself. My name's Julie."

He touched his hat brim, ready to leave. "Nice to meet you, ma'am."

"These clothes get dry, I may go over to Saint David. I'm tired of living like this."

"Yes, ma'am."

"I aim to get a divorce from him!" she shouted after him.

He nodded that he heard her and rode out to join Billie.

"She divorcing him?"

"I guess."

"Reckon she wanted you to know all about it." Billie chuckled as they rode down the wash. "Where's he at?"

"She said she didn't know."

"What now?"

"We go back to camp. Wait for Gray Fox and the soldiers to arrive."

She looked across the grassland that swept to the distant Chiricahuas. "All this country once belonged to them, didn't it?"

"I suppose it did. They held it. Why?"

"Just asking. I guess I'd fight hard, too, if they took my land."

They met Vi on the road coming back with the dead one wrapped in a blanket and the moaning Yost holding his arm in the back.

"Mayor Jackson is sending him to the jail in Tombstone." Slocum gave a head toss toward the wounded one.

"No one will miss him," Vi said and nodded at Billie. "What about Krier?"

"He wasn't home and his wife says she's divorcing him."

"Don't blame her. He's never treated her well. She about starves at times when he takes off and doesn't leave her anything to live on."

"Anyway, he wasn't there. Gray Fox back?" He tossed his head in the direction of the camp.

"Never seen any sign of him."

Slocum looked off toward the mine and the brown streaks of the waste dumped high on the mountainside. Where was the chief? Could this all be a trick to get them to watch his women and children until Geronimo was deep in Mexico and offered no threat to them? Then Fox'd go back to his free roaming along the Mexican border again. A notion he hadn't thought about before.

"I'll get him on to the mayor. And bring you a fresh quarter of beef day after tomorrow. Mary said that would be soon enough."

"Good, she'd know the needs," Slocum said and reined the roan aside. "Send me word if you hear in time of another raid."

"I never heard about the last one." Vi shook his head, taking up the reins. "But I sure will if I learn anything."

"Thanks."

Vi touched his hat brim and smiled big at Billie before he drove away. She about tore the buckskin's head off turning him around and then she looked hard-eyed at Slocum. "See what I mean?"

"I look hard at nice things, too."

"Aw—" She shook her head in disapproval, then sent the buckskin up the trail in the dry grass.

When they came in sight of camp, Mary came running to meet them.

"Someone has taken a young girl," she said.

"One of Geronimo's men?"

"We don't know. Deer is a teenager. She went to pick prickly pear fruit on the far mountain. There are lots of ripe ones there. When she didn't return, her mother went to see about her. All she found was a spilled basket of pears and horse tracks."

"Were they shod?" he asked swinging down.

"Yes, but the renegades have stolen several shod horses by now."

"Which way did they head?"

"Teyah, her mother, said she thought for the Whetstones."

"Find the mother a horse and have her take me up there. Maybe I can track them down."

"Here, take mine," Billie said and bolted out of the saddle. "I'll stay here. You be careful. There may be several of them."

"What does Deer look like?"

"She has wide eyes. She wore a gold coin on a rawhide thong and has a long scar on her left arm."

"No word from Fox?"

Mary shook her head.

"Is that usual?"

The woman pursed her lips, then she spoke. "They have ridden long distances to find food."

Or make a raid. He wondered about that as an option. The whites watch his people and feed them, while they pilfer and raid some small Mexican villages. Perfect for them. He ran with Mary and Billie for the camp.

Mary explained in Apache to the short women what he wanted to do for her. She nodded in approval and Billie helped her in the saddle. She blistered away giving him only a short moment to tell the two women to be on good guard—Krier was still on the loose.

He caught Teyah on the top of the first hill and she pointed across the next swale to the far hillside. She galloped the buckskin though the loose gravel path downhill as fast as she went uphill. With Slocum on her heels, she drew up at the sight of the basket on the ground.

"I find her basket here," she said in broken Spanish.

He nodded and dismounted to search the ground. Shod horse hooves were clear, so were a few boot heels. He pointed them out and she agreed.

"White men."

"Blanco hombres."

"*Si.* I will trail them, you go back to camp. If I can find her, I will bring her back."

"I should never have let her come over here alone, but she wanted some prickly pears to fix."

He nodded. "It's not your fault, there are such bad men in this land."

Sad-eyed, she looked up at him. "Please find her."

"If I can, I will." He looked off toward the purple Whetstones. Lots of tough country.

"Gracias."

6

He found a seep to water himself and the roan in the lower canyon. The gelding drank deep at the small pool in the rock basin. Slocum studied the steep sides dotted with junipers. Late afternoon shadows were beginning to submerge the east side of the mountain into a softer light. The tracks of the horses were still easy to follow. Too easy. He worried he might burst into them. They must have a place ahead with water for they didn't use this small spring when they passed within fifty feet of it.

In the saddle again, he rode up the trail and soon emerged on a flat bench. Standing in the stirrups, he tried to see any sign of them. Then a whiff of wood smoke and he shut the roan down. Colt in his hand, he dismounted, then led the horse and dodged around the bushy junipers. Voices carried.

He recognized one—Madison's. That sumbitch and some more were up ahead. He took the roan back a good distance and hobbled it in a patch of grass. Then he began his approach to their camp. Using the evergreens for cover he moved in closer.

On the ground, under the pungent-smelling boughs, he moved slow, with care. Through the boughs, he had took a good view at the bare half-moon-shaped ass of the ex-scout busy beating his meat.

"Hold that hellcat, boys," Madison said. "I'm getting this bastard up big enough, she'll strangle on it."

"You'd better hurry," someone said in Spanish as if holding her down required a great effort.

"*Si*, she is really wild," another complained as she thrashed around under them.

54

Slocum could see her brown legs kicking despite the two men's effort. His hand went to the butt of his Colt. From the corner of his eye, he spotted the fourth one with a rifle standing by smiling, amused at their efforts. Damn, he could have taken those three they were so busy getting ready to rape her. Number four made it tougher.

"Sorry, Deer—" escaped his lips in a silent whisper. Nothing he could do against those odds—besides, she might get shot in case of any gunplay.

"I got this for you, baby! Here! Take this!" Madison shouted.

Slocum saw his butt plunge forward and the loud shout from all of them as the rape began. The guttural sounds of Madison as he grunted away on top of her carried clear to him. Slocum ground his molars in anger, lying in the juniper needles—unable to do anything to stop the rape of Deer. It would be after dark before he could do a damn thing.

One of the holders jumped up and began wildly stroking his dick with an "I am next" enthusiasm.

Slocum wanted to blast all four of them. But she'd only get hurt in the gun fight. He was too late to save her from the savage experience. Maybe after dark he could extract her from their clutches.

He dared not move. His only chance for any success was catching them off guard. They were drinking whiskey out of the neck of a bottle being passed around and cheering the third man's efforts to fuck her. Obviously his dick wasn't hard for it kept coming out of her and he had to reinsert it.

"Ah, Bronco," someone said to the rifle holder. "You get fourths."

"I will make her scream."

"Ha, she didn't even scream when he popped her cherry."

The man smiled big and set down the rifle. "You boys have little pencil dicks. You will see." He took a big swallow of the whiskey and handed the bottle on in the dimming light.

Number three rammed his home and gave a great cry when he came inside of her.

The guard walked over and got on his knees. He reached up and came back with a handful of her juices to wipe on his big ram. Then he rolled her over on the blanket, drew her up on her knees and spread the cheeks of her butt apart.

Her screams shattered the twilight as he drove his rod into her.

Slocum was on his feet, ran over and busted the man over the head with his gun butt. He went down like a poled steer on top of the girl with a groan. One of the Mexicans, seated on the ground, went for his six-gun, but Slocum's spoke first. In the haze of the gun smoke, the second one ran away screaming, "Mother of God!"

Where was Madison? He pulled the groggy man off of her and she looked at him out of dollar-sized eyes.

"Teyah sent me," he said and jerked the naked girl to her feet. "Get the blanket."

He kept the Colt cocked as she fought getting the blanket. That damned Madison had to be around somewhere. No sign of him.

"My horse is downhill. Go that way!"

She obeyed him and disappeared. Gun ready, he backed to the juniper. Out of their sight and satisfied, he holstered his gun and ran down the slope after her blanket-wrapped figure. At the roan, he cut the rope hobbles in one slash, then boosted her in the saddle. He stepped in the stirrup, swung up behind her and they fled the scene. She arranged the blanket around her body as they fled.

Long past dark, they rode off the hillside into camp. He lifted her down and she thanked him in Spanish.

"Is she all right?" Mary asked as the women crowded around her.

"No," Slocum said. "But there was nothing I could do to stop them."

"She's alive."

He nodded.

"Come, I'll fix you some supper," Billie said and took his hand. "You haven't eaten all day."

He put an arm over her shoulder and they went to the campfires. Seated on the ground, he watched Billie's shapely butt in the skirt as she bent over and heaped his tin plate with meat and beans. Maybe later in her arms, he could forget about the bitter rape of Deer. It would haunt him for some time.

The coolness of dawn held back the eventual hard heat of the day ahead. A soft purple light arose beyond the Chiricahuas. A wave of goose bumps swept over his back and arms as he dressed. Already women worked down in the camp. He could hear the soft occasional clatter of tin pan or cup. He pulled on his boots, then buttoned his shirt. Billie was still asleep and he quietly left her to snooze. No problems in the night; he felt grateful and went to find some coffee.

Mary spotted him and poured a cup. She handed it to him when he reached her where the reflection of the fire's heat could be absorbed. Squatted on his boot heels, he blew on the coffee.

"How's the girl?" he asked.

"In time, she will be fine." Mary nodded in approval.

"Good. Nothing I could do to stop it until they were distracted. I didn't want her to get hurt."

"I understand. That happened to me my first day at the Indian School."

"You were how old then?"

"Eight or nine."

"Who did it?"

"A white teacher."

Slocum studied his coffee.

"That was not the last time either."

"You sure got a tough introduction to the white man's world." He looked at the short woman who stood so straight-backed. "I'm going back to look for them and Madison. But I hate to leave you all in camp without a man. Is Fox coming back?"

"He's had problems or he would be here by now. There's a small band that lived in Mexico and he was going to contact them."

"Do you know where they are at? Can you draw me a map?"

"Yes. But Lupe could lead you there."

"No—" He shifted his weight to his other leg. "She's the rifle shooter. You need her here in case of trouble. Draw me a map. I can go find them if they're alive. I'll have Clayton send down some guards from the mine."

"Why does he do all this for us?"

"He figures the better he treats you the less trouble for his mine."

She nodded she understood, standing with her arms crossed. "It is nice to see children with full bellies running about with energy."

"It is. I'm going up to the mine and talk to to Clayton. Then if he has some help he can spare, I'll go look for Fox and the others."

"I will have several of the women be lookouts."

"Yes, you can expect anything. Some crazy people in the world."

He went by and talked to the sleepy-eyed Billie, who sat up and squirmed under the blanket. "I'm going to ride up to the mine and speak to Clayton. Then I'm going to Mexico if he has some guards to spare and see about Gray Fox."

"I want to go along with you." She put the blouse on over her head, then stood and drew the skirt up her shapely bare legs and tied it at her waist

"Mexico is a tough place." He looked hard at her for an answer.

"I know. But I want to go along."

"We'll need some supplies. I'll go by the livery and buy a pack horse and get what we'll need on the way back, if Clayton can spare the man power."

She winked mischievously at him and began to roll up their bedding. "I hope he has the help."

Slocum left her, caught the roan and saddled him. In minutes, he was headed up the flat for the trail to the mine. He searched around several times after the last episode on the mountain; he wanted no repeat deals with ambushers. In a half hour, he reined up at the mill office and Clayton came out on the porch with a cup of coffee in his hand.

"Morning. How's things in camp down there?"

"A few problems we need to discuss."

"Them bucks come in?"

"No and that's another item to talk about."

"Come in. It sure sounds like things are not going like we planned. The damned army at Fort Bowie passed on the word for Fort Grant to send the escort. Word is they don't have any troops to send. They're all out looking for Geronimo."

Slocum told him about the abduction and also the Mexico business about Fox.

"What do you figure happened to him?" Clayton asked, leaning back in his swivel chair so the springs protested. He clasped his hands behind his head and scowled in disgust as he listened to Slocum. "And I thought this would be easy." He laughed.

"I'll make a quick trip down there if you can spare a few men to watch the camp."

"You want to leave soon, huh?"

"Yes, I need to run into Crystal Springs and get some supplies. Need a pack horse, too."

"Buz Allen is a good man. I'll send him and two more. I'll tell them two they need to be there at all times until you return."

"He be there by noon?"

"Yes. You be careful in Mexico. They shoot folks and ask questions later."

"I know it well."

"Sooner we can get all the Apaches here, the quicker they can be transferred."

Slocum agreed, shook the man's hand and headed for Crystal Springs. He arrived there and checked the sun's time. He'd need to be back at the camp in thirty minutes to meet the guards.

"Need a pack horse," he said to the livery man.

Grizzly-faced with his salt and pepper whiskers, the man spat his tobacco aside. "That bay can pack. I'd sell that paint cheap."

"What's cheap?"

"Ten bucks."

"What's he do?" Slocum was on the fence and looking hard at the mustang. He was a young horse, no need to mouth him.

"He'll kick the hell out of you getting on."

"Throw in a cross buck pack saddle?"

"Yeah, I'd like to see you put it on him." The livery man laughed.

Slocum bounded over the corral, then took a reata off the fence post and made a loop swinging it over his head. The paint gelding had merged in with the others and held his head up to see in the haze of dust stirred up. Singing like an attacking hawk cutting the air, the rawhide rope settled around his neck and Slocum's hand flew back cinching it tight.

The paint bucked a few times scattering the others. Slocum set his heels in the ground and jerked him around. Walking forward, he spoke softly as the paint blew rollers out his nose. He went to his right side and led him up to the fence where the expectant seller frowned.

"You got a damn way with horses, mister."

On the right side, Slocum applied the pad first. Then he took the cross buck from him and strapped it on. The paint saddled, he headed for the gate.

"Now how in the hell did you do that?"

"I'd tell you for ten bucks."

The man wiped his bristled mouth with his calloused palm looking in deep thought. "I'd give that to know. All right, you earned him. How did you do that?"

"He's an Indian pony. They get on the right side and saddle them from there."

"Sumbitch if that ain't so and I never thought about it. What's your name?"

"Slocum."

"Blister McCoy's mine. Ain't you the guy watching after them damn Apaches?"

"For now. The army's coming after them soon."

"Can't be too soon. My scalp itches just thinking they ain't over a mile a way." He was scratching his crotch again.

Slocum wanted to tell him a good bath and shampoo might help the itching, but he went on. No sense wasting his words on McCoy. A bath was the last thing on that man's mind.

He picked up the needed food supplies, an iron skillet, and coffeepot, plus some water bags. It could get dry in Mexico. A couple of tin plates to eat off of and some forks and spoons. That all packed in two large panniers, he carried his load out on the porch. He tied up the paint's left hind foot and put one pannier on him despite the horse's fussing around. The right one went on easy. Finally he loaded the left one and covered them with some new canvas and a diamond hitch. The foot catch released, he caught the lead, thanked the boy from the store for helping him and headed for the camp.

Only thing, the paint led reluctantly and he'd have Billie drive him until he understood to keep up. A day on the trail and he'd be fine. Couldn't look too close at a gift horse.

Billie came on the run to meet him. "What's his name?" she asked inspecting the paint.

"Wahoo, I guess."

He dismounted and she stepped in to hug him. "I was worried you might have trouble in town."

"Na, they're like old McCoy at the livery. All concerned the Apaches are so close."

"These women and children wouldn't hurt them."

"We know it, they don't. Let's find something to eat—" He looked around. "Clayton's men here yet?"

"I haven't seen them."

"They'll be along. We get some food and they should be here."

"Then we can leave for Mexico?"

"You having second thoughts?"

"No, I want to go with you."

"Fine, it won't be no picnic."

She hugged his arm. "Every night with you's been one."

He glanced down at her and chuckled.

While they ate beef and beans, Lupe drew him a map in the dirt of where the rancher was in the foothills south of the San Bernadino Springs. Slocum felt certain he could find the place. So thirty minutes after the guards arrived, Slocum told them what to watch for, introduced them to Mary and prepared to leave.

Buz Allen was a stocky built man, who carried a .44/40 Winchester like he knew every working part of it. He saluted them when they rode out and assured Slocum the camp would be safe. They left leading Wahoo. Billie's efforts with a quirt made him catch up to the roan in a long jog trot.

Slocum planned to cross the border on the San Pedro River bottoms, then swing east. If they moved fast they should be near the camp in a day—maybe a day and a half.

By sundown they made camp on the river, filled the water bags and hobbled the horses in the bloody sunset's light. She stripped down and then dove into the pool. Like a river otter, she surfaced and swept her hair back. "Water's just right. I sure miss rivers and creeks. We had lots of places to swim in Arkansas."

He toed off his boots and nodded. "Been there."

"You agree?"

"I agree." He pulled his shirt off over his head. A good relaxing swim and soaking might revive him. Then he shed his socks standing on one foot then the other. His gun belt set down, he dropped his pants and waded out in the water. Whew, the water did feel good. A small cool stream from a nearby spring blended with the tepid flow and made it relaxing.

She swam over and emerged dripping to stand before him. "Nice to have you to myself."

"I've been yours all along."

She wrinkled her nose looking up at him and reached out to cup his scrotum. "Not like this."

"First, I need to swim a little and get rid of some of this road dust."

She released him and made a pained face. "I'll drag up some driftwood and make a fire before it gets too dark to see."

"Good idea. I'll only be minute," he said and dove into the pool.

"No longer," she teased after him.

In the growing darkness, they sat naked to dry on the canvas cloth used to cover the pack. Shadows engulfed the land and the orange flames of their small fire danced on her proud, small breasts as she handed him some coffee.

"Like Adam and Eve in the garden of Eden," she said and smiled, pleased.

"Like that." He blew on the coffee. "But I am afraid we'll be thrown out of it tomorrow."

"Maybe—" Then she drew up her bare legs and hugged them as she laughed. "And we'll need fig leaves, too."

"Lots of them."

She dropped her hands back and braced herself. "I could stay here forever."

"Forever is a long time."

With her eyes closed, she crawled over and climbed on his lap. He set the coffee aside and raised her chin up to kiss her. Their mouths met and the magic began like a symphony. The first sounds came like booms of thunder and the world of passion swallowed them both. Hot mouths seeking each other. Her rock hard nipples teased by his calloused palm massaging them, until he lifted her up and began to suck and consume them. Her small fingers combed through his too-long hair as she pressed her breasts to him.

His finger began to probe though her stiff pubic hair and she widened her knees for his entry. The moist ring began to swell as he found the rising clit and she gasped for breath. Then suddenly, he stopped and listened.

Something was out there. He swung past her and reached for the Colt.

"What is it?"

"I heard a horse snort. He's not ours," he whispered.

"What do we do?" She drew on her blouse and then squirmed into her skirt.

"Be quiet." He pulled on his pants, then his boots without socks. On his knees, he began his search. The cicada music was loud. A few bullfrogs downstream croaked and he listened— there was someone or something out there.

7

Six-gun in his hand, he eased himself up and in a crouch moved toward the horses. They might be horse thieves. Then a stallion whistled and stomped the ground. Who in the hell was out there? He held his hand back to keep Billie from harm's way. Not seeing anything near the horizon like the outline of the horses, he tried to listen and locate the direction the sounds came from.

Goose bumps popped out on back of his arms and he shivered as he paused to hear above the night insect's buzzing. Overhead, a million stars pricked the night and a quarter moon hung in the south, so the light was precious to see by, except in the bare grassy areas. Every muscle in his body from his trigger finger to his legs was like a spring ready to surge.

They huddled, squatted on the ground in sight of their horses, which appeared to be looking at something in the south. He trusted the keen senses of a horse; times before they had saved him from bounty men creeping up on his camp. Whoever it could be must be in that direction.

"Friend or foe?" he shouted in Spanish.

No answer.

Were they Apaches? A white man might answer; an Indian, doubtful, especially one with murder on his mind. Not like an Apache to be out and about in the night though; they were too superstitious about being killed after sundown and their spirit ending up in never-never land. Still, someone was out there.

"Que esta?" came the reply.

"Ride in closer and keep your hands in the open," he ordered.

"Ah, senor, we worried you were Apaches."

Two men rode into view, both wore sombreros.

"Who are they?" she whispered.

"Damned if I know, but be on your guard," he said in a soft voice over his shoulder.

"My name is Benito Mendoza. This is my man, Phillipe." He rode up on the high-stepping stud.

Slocum acknowledged the two and watched close as they dismounted with a ring from their spurs.

"I am traveling to see my cousin in Tucson." Mendoza gave the reins to his man and then removed his sombrero and bowed. "*Gracias* for receiving us."

"No problem."

"This is the senora?"

"That's Billie," he said. "She's going to build the fire up."

"My pleasure," Mendoza said to her. "Hobble the horses and come on," he said to his man.

"Traveling late at night, aren't you?"

"We wanted to stop at a small village called San Dias, but there were men there I did not trust—obvious banditos, so we rode on quickly."

"Dangerous business, traveling the roads. Apaches, bandits and greedy-minded individuals."

"Ah, *si*, but I promised my cousin I would come to see her and her husband."

"Have a seat," Slocum said.

"We obviously disturbed your sleep."

"We're up now. What is the news about the Apaches?"

"The *federales* captured several of them."

"Whose band?"

"Gray Fox, I think they call him."

Slocum let the words shed off like a light rain. "I've heard of him. Where do they have them?"

"Arrido."

"Lot's of *federales?*"

Mendoza shook his head. "Only a small company, but they must have caught them sleeping. Captain DeBaca waits for more troops to move them to prison."

"He must be a good soldier."

Mendoza shook his head. "I think he was lucky. The Apaches had little ammunition, I heard."

"So when will the other soldiers arrive?"

"Oh, who knows? In Mexico, things move slow like an ant."

They both laughed. Mendoza handed him a small cigar. "Let us each smoke, then we can sleep a few hours."

Slocum did not miss the man looking at Billie across the firelight. But it was only a look of admiration and Phillipe squatted a few feet back as if waiting his patron's next orders.

The small cigars were strong and they smoked them down, talking about the rains that did not come and the market for cattle. Mendoza spoke of his own rancher and how the threat of the roaming Apaches made making a profit so hard.

"Ah, this one they call Geronimo brings me much trouble. Maybe he is out of ammunition, too?"

"Who would know?"

Mendoza thanked him at the end of the cigar and went off a ways to where Phillipe had spread his bedroll. Slocum listened to the coyotes yapping at the setting moon, then he joined Billie. Already the temperature had begun to drop.

"What will we do? They have him prisoner," she whispered, when he crawled in beside her warm, naked body.

He rose up and fit his hips between her legs. His prick slid in her gates and she sighed. "That can wait till later," he whispered in her ear, pumping his aching butt into her. "Much later."

"Yes," she sighed and quickly raised herself off the blanket high enough to receive all of him.

His mind absorbed in the pleasure of her small subtle body and the thickening walls of her pussy, he pushed on to a new point in their pleasure. The friction increased his heart rate and the swirl of their passion released him from his earthly problems.

Soon their breathing reached a crescendo and the fury of their lovemaking became a raging fire. He moved hard into her. His cannon blasted the red-hot cum and they collapsed into exhausted unconsciousness.

Dawn, Billie was up, squatted at the fire making flour tortillas in the skillet with her fingers. Her frijoles were heating in the pot. Phillipe sat on his haunches and spoke to her in his broken English. "I hate making them. Mine never turn out."

"They are fine. You are a widow?" He took a tortilla in his hand at her urging and put the cooked frijoles down on it then deftly rolled it into a burrito.

"Apaches killed my husband, Fred." She motioned for Slocum to help himself as she hand patted out another tortilla with a scowl at her handiwork.

"They are such bad people."

"Yes. Slocum here has taken me in."

"You in?" Phillipe, with his mouth full, frowned at her.

"Hired me."

"Oh, *si*. He is your patron."

Slocum shook his head, filling his tortilla and said in Spanish. "I work for her."

"Oh, *si*." Phillipe's eyes lighted up and he laughed.

"What did you tell him?" she asked, cutting her glare around at Slocum.

"I worked for you."

She shook her head in disapproval, turning over another tortilla in the pan.

His silver spur rowels ringing like bells, Mendoza joined them. Phillipe moved back.

"Ah, we have food." He smiled big and bowed for her. "So good to see you in the daylight, my lovely lady."

She blushed and indicated the food. "Not much, but plenty of it."

"Ah, a feast for a king. You must come by my hacienda. I would repay you ten times for your hospitality."

"What is the name of your rancheria?"

"I call it Los Doves for all the white winged ones that winter there," he said.

"Someday I'd love to see it." On her feet, she filled everyone's coffee cup.

"*Grand rancho*," Phillipe said, bobbing his head in approval over the food he consumed.

Slocum loaded Wahoo and saddled their horses while she broke camp. He shook hands with Mendoza and Phillipe and boasted Billie in the army saddle. Then they parted and he studied the greasewood and cactus as they trotted southeast. Gray Fox was a prisoner of the Mexican military—another problem for him to solve.

"I know it's on your mind. What will you do about it?" she asked, giving Wahoo a few licks with the quirt to make him keep up with the roan.

"We'll need to look over the situation and see what we can do about it. Maybe we can't do anything. If they ship them off to prison, they'll probably die there."

She booted the buckskin up beside him. "I don't see you letting that happen."

"Hey, I don't have an army. We're just going down here to look things over."

The straw hat she wore was pushed up on her head, the chin string drawn under her jaw. She raised up and laughed.

"My brothers were always easygoing. Never got in a hurry, like Fred; they always planted things late. But you're like my Grandpaw Shanks. He always had his crop in early and weeds never took it. Come harvest he had the best. When he set in to do something, he done it right."

Slocum smiled at her. "But the *federales* are tough."

"The only thing tough in Mexico is this saddle and those cactus."

"We'll see."

She twisted in the saddle and then turned back. "Reckon his ranch is that nice?"

"You looking for a roof over your head?"

"Girl's got to keep open all her options. You said you'd have to ride on one day."

He nodded and studied the day's heat waves as they began to rise and distort the desert and purple saw-edged mountains ahead. He hardly considered Mendoza a find and he might have a wife at home. But Billie was a realist about the matter of him leaving her some time in the future.

"Why must you run?"

"A long time ago, a sorry loser came back in a saloon and tried to shoot me. He was hardly more than boy. I tried to talk him out of it. He died."

"But that was self-defense."

"His grandfather is a rich man. He keeps two Kansas deputies looking for me full-time."

She shivered despite the hot sun and hugged her arms. "I couldn't stand to always be looking behind my back."

"Gets to be a way of life after a while."

"I guess so. How'll I know them when I see them?"

"One rides a big Appaloosa horse with a white blanket on his butt with black rosettes. The Abbott brothers are always easy to spot. Big loudmouths."

"Easy enough to spot then?" she asked.

He agreed and they rode on. That was when she told him she wasn't making any more tortillas. Chuckling first, he finally laughed. "Don't make any more then."

"I won't."

It was after dark when they rode into Arrido. They ate supper cooked by an old woman in the street. Peppers, beans and beef wrapped in a freshly made, blanket-sized flour tortilla.

"Good?" the toothless woman asked, looking up at him in the dim light from the cantina's doors.

"Very good," he told her. "Where do they keep those Apaches?"

"Oh." She waved her thin hand toward down the street. "In the old livery stables. I worry much they will escape and cut all of our throats."

"Aren't there many soldiers guarding them?"

"Ha, drunks and convicts—all worthless, and they go about the streets like fighting cocks." She shook her head wearily. "I'll be glad when they are all gone. The *federales* and the Apaches."

"We'd better put our horses up and get a room. I need to do some scouting," he said privately to Billie.

"You figure how many horses it will take to get them out of here?"

"Plenty, but I need to see how many are prisoners."

"Ain't that dangerous?" She frowned under the hat.

"No, I'm a curious gringo who wants to see what real Apaches look like."

"That make sense. Where will we stay?"

"What inn is the best to stay at?" he asked the old woman.

"Deloris Castele's. It is on the right." She waved her hand in the direction. "She has a corral for the horses in back."

He thanked her and they led their horses past several cantinas where the music and laughter of the *putas* drifted into the dark street. The sign hung out read: DELORIS'S INN.

A buxom woman came in the lobby and greeted them. In minutes they were assigned a room and a boy, for a dime, took their horses to put them up. Slocum explained about Wahoo and satisfied the boy understood him, he followed Billie to the room.

Double French doors opened to a small garden area that reeked of roses and bougainvillea. He stood in the doorway and considered his next move looking at the distant stars. Damn *federales* always were tough even staffed with convicts. Maybe even made them tougher than drafted boys.

"What will you do?"

"Go see what I can learn. Can you shoot a gun?"

"Sure, why?"

"I want you armed. I have a small .30 caliber cap and ball revolver that is loaded—five shots. You may need to use it down here."

He put the small pistol in her hand and closed her fingers around it. "I'll be back in a few hours. Don't shoot me."

She laughed. "You be careful."

He kissed her and went out into the night. A while later, standing in the alley across the street from the old livery stables, he spotted a uniformed guard on duty at the big double doors. Another was busy feeling the breasts of a *puta* in the shadows. They lounged on the ground. His arm over her shoulder, he blew in her ear, then stuck his other hand under her dress. She shoved the dress down to keep herself from being exposed and turned her face up for him to kiss her.

In minutes, the guard obviously had his middle finger in her pie for she spread her legs apart for him. He was on his knees, thrusting his finger in and out of her. He tore his pants open, shoved her down, then quickly smothered her under his body, haunching himself into her despite her protests about being in the dirt.

The other guard checked around, then set his rifle against the wall. He whipped out his dick and began to jack off. The first one gave a great grunt and came. His pal pulled him back by the shoulder. "My turn."

The first one sat on his butt in an obvious daze. The *puta* tried to protest, but number two shoved her back on the ground and moved in to mount her. "Not till I am done with you."

"Cheap bastards," she swore and then groaned when he hefted his rod into her.

In the darkness, Slocum walked on the opposite sidewalk of

flat rocks and went south along the building fronts. He cut across the street, slipped between a building and came out in the back. He had some time if those two were the only sentries. He needed to see if he could talk to the Apaches. At the rear door, he lifted the bar holding the door. The door squeaked on the hinges. He stopped it and held still—he heard nothing from the two on guard.

"Gray Fox," he hissed.

"Here," a voice from the pitch darkness.

"Are you in chains?"

"Yes."

In seconds, he was squatted beside the chief who was seated on the floor of the stables. Dim light came through a window opening, so he could check the chain. They wore legs irons riveted on them and connected by short lengths.

"If I get you a file, can you file off these rivets so it can be knocked through?"

"Yes."

"We must be careful. They'll get suspicious. I'll never get all of you out of here."

"The women and children?"

"Safe and well fed."

"Good."

Slocum nodded. He needed a file. There might be one in the building; many times blacksmiths worked in such places. He nodded to the tools lined up in a row. The smell of coal filled his nose and he smiled at his discovery. There had to be a file over there. His hands touched the tools, long-handled tongues, then his fingers felt a file's coarse surface. One and a piece of one—good.

Back at Fox's place, he showed him how how to use the tool, then used the rat tail to poke out the rivet. They exchanged a smile. Slocum went and found a board, he cut off a sliver with his jack knife and jammed it in the hole for the rivet.

Gray Fox nodded in appreciation. "Good until we all are free, huh?"

"Hide the shavings, too."

He used his hand to blend them in the manure dust. "I need to find enough horses. I'll be back tomorrow night. Be sure they don't fall off."

"What do they call you?"

"Slocum."

"You are the man from Crystal Springs?"

"One of them."

"*Ussen* be with you."

Slocum nodded ready to leave. He listened for the guards and the *puta* who was arguing with them out in front. "Be ready to go tomorrow night."

Two dozen pairs of dark eyes followed him and heads bobbed in agreement, then he slipped out the back door, replaced the bar and drew a deep breath. He still needed lots of mounts and he needed to have them ready. Apaches could ride bareback, but still the numbers looked big. And so many horses he'd need to assemble and not alert the *federales*. He eased himself between the building to the front and headed for his place in the alley where he could observe the sentries.

From there he could see Number Two had the *puta* down on her knees sucking his cock. He held her head in a fistful of her hair and she mumbled in protest.

"Suck harder, you little bitch." Then with a bow in his back, he must have come. She pulled back, gasping for her breath, pushing him away.

8

He woke up with a swollen bladder and got up to piss in the night jar. The answer to the horse problem was cut in half by a new solution. One could ride, one could run. He knew Apaches had done that before and outrun the cavalry. Finished pissing, he went to the half-open doors and listened to the first birds of morning singing and the distant cries of the early morning street peddlers out in front of the inn.

"What do we do today?" she asked, sitting up on the bed and hugging her knees.

"Locate a dozen horses. I found Fox and have him filing off the rivets on their leg irons—I hope."

"What then?"

"We charge up, spring them and run away."

"But the army?"

"We steal their horses, so they can't follow us."

She stretched her arms over her head. The sheet slipped away and her pointed breasts were thrust forward. With a crooked smile for him and a wink, then she bounced out of bed and came over to hug him.

"And we can play all day in bed?"

"Nice idea, but we'd better scout their horses and learn all we can about the situation here."

She tugged on his arm, pulling him toward the bed. "So we don't take all day."

Shaking his head, he trailed along on his bare feet across the tile floor. "I've awoken a demon."

"Yes, yes."

She stood on the bed and threw her arms around his neck and began kissing him, pressing her still-warm body against his skin. He forgot all about the plight of the Apaches and anything else as his desire for her body exploded in his brain.

An hour later, from a distance, they looked over the cavalry's horses. Sleek, grain-fed, they were tied in a face-to-face row at a rope hitch line. Privates were busy brushing them down and inspecting their hooves, cleaning out the packed manure and being sure the shoes were on tight. The ones needing a farrier's attention were backed out and led to the forge being kept alive by a sweaty-faced private on the bellows.

"Who guards them?" she asked, behind her hand.

"Soldiers."

"How many?"

"A few, I think. Two soldiers is all that guard the Apaches." He leaned his shoulder to the adobe wall and studied the fancy coach that passed. A dark-eyed senorita fanned herself with a pleated red fan, seated in the rear bench. Her thick eye lashes and serious look caught his attention for a second then she was gone. Some rich hacienda owner's coach window framed her creamy coffee-colored face.

"She must be rich," Billie said.

"Very rich," he said, satisfied they could take the horses, which were only a block away from the temporary prison.

"Wonder what that's like?" she asked as they sauntered up the flagstone sidewalk, past several shops. Gunsmiths, saddle makers, dry goods and others. Street traffic included noisy ungreased axle ox carts, burros packed with sticks for firewood or water, delivery cans and riders on mustangs and burros.

No sign of the fancy red coach. They passed on the far side of the street from the livery where they held the Apaches. Two more on-duty guards different from the ones the night before stood at the closed double doors. Obviously the *federales* had conscripted the building for the time being to hold them. The village probably had only a small jail for an occasional out-of-hand drunk, a person that went insane or a criminal.

"What what's like?" he finally answered her, so busy in his own thoughts about the layout.

"Oh, being so rich."

"They aren't much different from other folks. Except they have to worry about how to keep it instead of how to make it."

"I guess you're right. But I'd switch places with them."

"No, you'd have to dress fancy all the time."

"Sure, people expect the rich to be well-dressed."

They ordered some bean and chicken burritos from a street vendor. The vendor knelt beside the small firebox and griddle, deftly making the first large flour tortilla in her hands while they waited.

Slocum glanced away as if disinterested when the two officers rode past them. One was a captain, the other, a young lieutenant, fresh from the academy at Mexico City. His superior wore a pencil-thin mustache and rode like he had a broom handle stuck up his ass. The younger man had a less certain look in his eye.

"*Federales*." The woman spit in the gutter and made a bad face.

"You don't like them?" he asked in a soft voice, being certain no one could hear him, but the woman was busy turning the first tortilla with her fingertips, peeling it up and then turning it over on the grill.

"I hate them. They rape the women and run over the men in this village like they own it all."

"Maybe they do."

"Maybe someday they will all get a gun barrel stuck up their asses, too."

Slocum winked at Billie. "You hate them?" he asked the woman.

"More than that—"

"One day the people will run Mexico, not the *federales* and not those Mexico City banditos."

Quickly, she filled the tortilla in her hand and then wrapped it. "Here, senora."

"*Gracias*," Billie said and took it in both hands. "It's hot and there's lots to eat."

"Good for you." The woman smiled up at her then put Slocum's tortilla on the grill. "You can use a little fat." She slapped her own rump. "Men like a little more back there than you got now."

They laughed at her words and when she finished his wrap, he thanked and paid her. They drifted down the street, enjoying their spicy breakfast and finally having coffee at a sidewalk cafe.

Three soldiers appeared and Slocum knew in an instant the two of them were the center of their attention. The strapping sergeant stopped and folded his arms before him.

"Gringo, the captain wishes to talk to you," said a broad-shouldered man built like a bull with a bushy mustache.

"I suppose I say no and you will take me anyway."

The noncom nodded.

"Billie, I shall return." He handed her some folded money and nodded to the three soldiers. "I'm coming."

"What do they want you for?" Billie asked.

"I have no idea. But I am sure we can discuss it later."

"Yes," she said, chewing on her lower lip.

Slocum nodded to the bull and waited for him to lead the way. "See you later."

When he went by the street vendor he heard the woman spit after their passage. It was hard to stop a smile.

"My name is Slocum."

"Franco," the noncom grunted.

"Well, Sergeant Franco, what is the captain's name?"

"DeBaca."

"I guess you guys have lots of work to do."

"We captured the Apache Chief Fox and his men."

"That must have been a big deal."

He motioned for Slocum to cross the street and head over to a jacal with guards at the doors. "We'll get that bastard Geronimo next."

Franco went past the private at the desk, leaned in the doorway and saluted someone. "*Mi capitán*, the gringo who calls himself Slocum is here."

"Send him in."

Franco saluted the man, then waved Slocum through the doorway.

"Ah, senor," DeBaca said, rising to introduce himself and shake hands. "So good to meet you. Have a seat."

Slocum sat in one of the two captain's chairs facing the desk.

"I guess you wonder why I have asked you here?"

"Yes, I do."

"We get many filibusters up here and I needed to know the nature of your business in Sonora." DeBaca leaned back in his chair and tented his fingers.

"I buy some cattle to export. You know Senor Don Lopez in Narcorza?"

DeBaca shook his head.

"He has a large hacienda down there. I have bought many head of cattle from him."

"How many can you use?"

"Three- and four-year-olds?"

"Yes."

"Five hundred head. Do you have some cattle?"

"No, but I need some money to finance feeding these red devils I am holding. I may tax all the ranchers and have them deliver me the beef."

"Oh, the only way I could pay for such animals is at the border. Otherwise they might claim them back."

"Where on the border and how much would you pay?"

"Ten dollars a head."

"Oh, no, you want to steal them."

"Fifteen and two dollars a head for the younger ones."

"You are a real cattle buyer." DeBaca laughed and nodded his approval. "I was only testing you. I believe you are here in Mexico to buy cattle."

"That's how I make my living."

"Much success. I feel sorry for the ones you deal with. You may go now."

"You get a herd, let me know." Slocum rose.

"No way, I would find a less experienced man to sell them to." DeBaca laughed again.

Slocum left the DeBaca's headquarters and walked down the busy street, wondering if Billie had gone back to their room in the inn. She stepped out of a store, looked hard at his back trail, then joined him.

"What was that all about?" she asked in a whisper.

"He wanted to know why I was here."

"What did you tell him?"

"I was buying cattle."

She nodded. "Good answer. I hope we get out of here tonight."

"So do I, but we're maybe being watched."

"What do we do about that?"

"Lose them."

"I have a feeling you've done this before."

"A few times."

They went back to the sidewalk cafe. The waiter, an older man, looked around to be certain no one was in earshot. "I will be glad to see those *federales* leave this town. They think they are the King of Spain." He snorted up his nose and wiped off the table. "This is Mexico now. We don't need them."

"You hear when they're leaving?" Slocum asked.

"No. They have sent for more soldiers; they want Geronimo, too."

"But why hold the others here?"

"Some kind of plan the captain has to lure Geronimo in here and ambush him."

Slocum chuckled and shook his head at the stupidity of such a plan. "Geronimo won't ever come here for them."

"Oh, the big captain thinks so."

Slocum and Billie lounged away the afternoon and after supper went back to their room.

"I want you to take my money." He dug it out of his boot vamp. "Isn't much, but if anything goes wrong, go back to Arizona. Don't stop. They will torture and rape you. They're cruel and vicious men."

He counted the paper money on the bed. A hundred and thirty dollars. "Not a fortune but I won't need it if I fail. You get your butt back up there. DeBaca is no one to deal with. Especially a woman."

"You worry me," she said, sitting cross-legged on the bed and taking the money he handed her.

"I hope I do."

"I know, head for the border as fast as I can."

He leaned over and kissed her. "That's my girl."

She closed her eyes and shook her head. "If anything happens to you—"

"Yes, you can go on. Do it. Those that survive must carry the cross. Go help Mary and the Apache dependents."

In the livery, a gun barrel poked Slocum's back as the latch fell in place. "Don't move."

His heart stopped. A fucking trap. He'd stepped into one like a dumb animal and the steel jaws were about to close on him with a big snap.

"Light the lamp," Sergeant Franco ordered. "We now know the gringo's real business here."

The brilliance of the candle lamp blinded him for a few seconds. But he could see there were no Apaches in the stable.

"You did us a big favor, Senor Slocum." Franco stood with his arms folded and smiled like he was pleased.

"How's that?" he asked, as the private holding the pistol on him removed Slocum's six-gun.

"The Apaches have slipped away to join Geronimo." Franco laughed. "We can track them right to his lair. And they think you turned them loose." He laughed some more and so did the handful of guards.

"You must have found the files for them. I left them here thinking they'd find them. Dumb Injuns—it took a gringo to show them how."

The skin crawled on the back of his neck. What did they plan to do to him?

"And for aiding the Apache murderers, you can go to Yucatan and work with them in the mines"—Franco reached drown and fondled the crotch of his pants—"while I screw that little bitch you brought with you."

They all laughed.

"Private Gomez go to the inn and get her," Franco said in a cold voice that chilled the stuffy air in the livery to ice. "You rape her before I do and I will cut your privates off. You hear me?"

"*Si*, sergeant." The young soldier ran off to obey the noncom.

"Ah, we will have fun with her. And she will bring a good price in a Mexico City brothel when we are done with her here. They like those white-skinned ones."

"Gray Fox will never lead you to his gold mine," Slocum said. "You boys still need me."

"What gold mine?" Franco's eyes danced with greed in the flickering light. "They had no ammo when we captured them. If they had a gold mine, why did they not have any ammo?"

"It was against their religion to take gold from the Madres. But they ran out of ammo and could not steal any, so they were going to that mine for more gold when you caught them."

"They had no gold." Franco shook his head and scowled.

"They have a rich mine some gringos found. They killed them and covered the mine entrance, so only they could find it."

"But you said their religion—"

"Even religious soup gets thin when you need ammunition and money to buy clothing and food."

"You're saying they were taking you to the mine?"

"They needed someone to sell it for them. Apaches aren't dumb. They know the value of money."

"Why were you here then?"

"I heard in Arizona that the *federales* had arrested them. So to protect my interest I came down here."

Franco narrowed his eyes. "How can you help me?"

"If I escape and join them, you can follow us to the mine."

"What do you get out of this?"

"My life?"

"I don't know. Sounds phony as hell. But you may have a point." He stepped over and waved a finger in Slocum's face. "You double-cross me and you're dead. Dead! Dead!"

"I savvy dead. You need a pension?"

"*Si.*"

"Gray Fox has that pension." Slocum gave a head toss toward the east.

"Senor! Captain?" someone was shouting hysterically at the guards in the street.

"Go find out what that sumbitch wants." Franco shook his head in disgust and waited as the soldier ran to open the front doors.

"Sergeant," the soldier shouted back. "This man he says that the gringo woman shot Private Gomez and has escaped."

Franco's eyes narrowed hard looking with a question at Slocum.

"What can I say? She's a hellcat."

9

Somehow by the next morning, Franco convinced DeBaca to stay at Arrido. The noncom and six soldiers rode with Slocum for the Madres. They needed him to show them the way up there and to negotiate with the Apaches so they could take over the mine.

He knew bits and pieces about Billie's escape. She'd shot the private in the leg—obviously aimed low—and then she vanished. Of course, they were looking for a small attractive woman and she no doubt by this time was wearing men's clothing a size or two too big. He could almost smile about her disguise, but he didn't dare in the company of the suspicious soldiers and their sergeant.

His plan was to catch the soldiers off guard and then escape. But before he left, he planned of finding out why the soldiers weren't tracking the escaped Apaches to Geronimo. Franco was the main concern and he wasn't easy fooled—only greed got the better of him.

Slocum twisted in the saddle. In addition to the horses, a half-dozen big pack mules came at the rear of the column churning dust up that any Apache could see from miles away. No telling where Gray Fox went—probably the Madres before he snuck back north. Franco could easily outrun the Injuns in the open desert. But once they were in the Madres, the soldiers would lose any pursuit and the Apaches would laugh at them from high bluffs. What did Geronimo once tell a newspaper reporter? "We used rocks on the Mexican army, but we saved our bullets for the American ones."

Getting away from Franco would not be easy. He wished he had a clear-cut plan, but he couldn't since he didn't know when his window of opportunity would arise; instead, he had to be ready to bail out whenever the time came.

Midday they arrived at a small tank surrounded by dead and live cottonwoods. An oasis with hundreds of birds singing while the hot wind rattled the leaves in the canopy overhead where the chorus resided. Siesta break. They gnawed on peppery beef jerky and then prepared to take naps. Franco left two men awake to guard things. Slocum didn't miss the noncom's suspicious cut of a hard look at him. Ignoring him, Slocum rolled out the blanket assigned him and used the time to sleep.

Franco could stay awake and be concerned about him—he could get the rest. He'd need a firearm, too, before he left this merry band. He drifted off and only too soon got a boot in his ribs that awoke him.

"Get ready to go."

"Sure," Slocum said and sat up. He rubbed his eyes and looked at the tank. Some Sonora doves bathed in the shallows, splashing and fluttering with each other. They reminded him of his youth, growing up in Alabama, swimming naked in Yabooty Creek with Carl and Fred Swain. At an age when boys' minds were full of questions about their own bodies and the opposite sex.

"You know old Fred got his finger in Lucy Grimes," Carl said, swimming backwards, sure his year older brother couldn't hush him as he back pedaled across the large hole of water.

"What was it like?" Slocum asked, ready to use the rope tied in the high sycamore limb to drop out in the middle of the pool.

"Kinda like her mouth felt sucking on my pecker."

Slocum knew his eyes had flown open at the sixteen-year-old's admission. On the other bank, Carl looked shocked by the words. Water dripping off him, he slung his wet hair out of his face and shook his head at Slocum. "Gawdamn you, Fred, you never told me about that."

"You never asked me."

"You telling us she sucked you off?" Slocum leaned on the rope.

"She sure did and I thought my balls were going to pop off in her mouth when I came."

Slocum took ahold of the rope, ran backwards, then raised his legs and went far out in the air. He let go and hit the water like a cannonball.

"You're a damn liar!" Carl shouted, bailed in and the fistfight was on.

It took all of Slocum's strength to separate them. Shouting and cussing at them, he finally got them apart.

"Aw, Carl's pissed cause he thinks she's so nice." Fred backed off and swam away.

"That sumbitch—" Carl seethed in rage. "She never sucked him off."

"Wait, why would he lie to us?" Slocum asked.

"Cause he knows it will piss me off."

"No more fighting, we'll all get put on strict quarters."

"All right," Carl agreed.

Slocum looked at Fred.

"I won't."

"Gringo!" Franco shouted, "Are you listening to me?"

Slocum turned in the saddle and nodded. "Guess I was thinking about that gold."

"So have I. We have to meet my scouts who have been trailing the Apaches at the Campos Hacienda. It is only a short ride north of here. Remember, no tricks, or I will kill you."

"Your party." He reined the roan northward on the wagon tracks, and Franco nodded in approval. Campos Hacienda, he knew nothing about it.

The palms marked the spot, he felt certain, two hours later when they trotted over a rise and the heat waves distorted his vision. Past the small irrigated fields of corn, beans and melons, they entered an open gate in the mud wall and rode into the water well–dominated square. Slocum felt ready for a drink when he spotted the red coach—the same one the dark-eyed lovely senorita rode in. Might be some good scenery in this place after all. He dismounted heavily and his sea legs held him. Damn, he needed a plan to get away from this bunch.

10

"Ah, Sergeant Franco, *mi amigo*," a short man in a white suit shouted and rushed out to greet them.

Slocum dismounted heavily and pulled down the crotch in his pants. He was ready for some rest and relaxation time. But obviously that was at the wishes of Franco. An ear turned toward their conversation, he loosened the cinches on his saddle.

"Ah, Franco, *si*, your scouts were here two days ago. They rode on."

"I told them to meet me here. What did they say they would do?"

"They said the Apaches were traveling fast—" Slocum could not hear any more of the man's words.

"Stupid bastards, they'll get caught in a trap."

"We staying here or what?" Slocum asked Franco.

"Oh, you can stay the night," the patron said. "Your horses need feed and rest. Your men look tired."

"All right. Romero take his horse and the other one to the stable. Senor Campos, this is Slocum." Franco looked pained.

"My pleasure, senor." Campos stuck out his hand.

"Mine, too," Slocum said, shaking it.

"We're going to the cantina and wash down some trail dust. The rest of you men be ready to ride at four A.M." Franco checked that each man had nodded and they understood his orders. "You stay with me," he said to Slocum and started for the bar.

"What is your business in Mexico?" Campos asked, walking with them.

"He's a supplier. The army needs something, he finds it," Franco said and Slocum nodded.

"Oh, good," Campos said and they went inside the sour-smelling cantina with a strong tobacco smoke aroma in the air.

"Ah, Sergeant Franco," the bartender said, coming from the back. "And you have a new friend."

"Slocum," Franco said and pointed to a bottle on the back bar. "What're you having?" he asked Slocum.

"A beer is fine."

The man set one glass and the bottle Franco asked for before him, then nodded and went to the tap for the beer. "Did you bring any rain?"

Franco shook his head and laughed on his way to a side table. "No rain, hombre. More dry weather."

"Ah, we end one drought and start another without a drop." He set the beer on the counter and Slocum started to dig for a coin.

"No, senor. Franco buys here."

Slocum shrugged, took his mug to the table and sat across from the noncom.

"How far away are we?" Franco asked, holding his half-full glass up ready to take a drink.

"Two, three days, hard riding."

Franco's hand, covered in black hair, was wrapped around the bottle. No telling how many fights this man had seen or been in. "That means four or five, huh?"

"Hard to say. The going gets tougher."

"Ambushes easier?"

Slocum nodded and raised the beer to his mouth. He hated tepid beer, but there damn sure was no ice this far south—they probably didn't even know what it was.

"You heard I was upset about the scouts going on."

"*Si.*"

"They'll get ambushed."

Slocum nodded.

"The gringo army had officers with their scouts. I met that Captain Crawford that got shot. He was tough as any Apache." Franco shook his head. "Mexico has no officers like that. DeBaca sits in his hotel room and screws young whores and doesn't get his boots dirty."

"You think that's why you can't control the Apaches?"

"Can you control the fucking wind?"

"No."

Franco laughed aloud. "See you and I have more in common than DeBaca has."

"I see what you mean."

"Campos will invite us to his house for supper soon."

"Me?"

"Oh, yes, cause you are a businessman."

Slocum nodded.

"But when you see his daughter, Juanita, your balls will ache for her."

Slocum simply agreed. From the cameo of her in the coach window he'd seen enough to know about her beauty.

"Ah, there you are," Campos said, coming through the batwing door. "I went to the stables and made sure your horses were rubbed down and fed grain. Supper is at seven. I know you have no clothes to dress up. So be comfortable. I will see the two of you then?"

Franco rose and toasted him. "*Gracias*, senor, we will be there." Then when the man left, he sat down. "I told you so. Stay in this bar. They've got a *puta* I need to see in the back." He rubbed his hand over his crotch as if checking it out. "Don't try nothing."

"I'm here at your disposal."

"See you stay that way." He used his hand to push himself up and spoke to the bar man. "Rosa here?"

"Second room."

"Good." Franco made a last frown at Slocum. Then like an ape, he stalked over to the blanket doorway and disappeared.

Slocum waited. A small boy ran buckets of beer to the soldiers. From the batwing doors, he could view the square and hear the music. Obviously the soldiers were having a fiesta, too. Don Campos treated the *federales* like kings. There was a reason for that much "gratitude," too.

"More *cerveza*?" the barman asked.

Slocum shook his head and watched the women cross the square with wet wash in baskets on their head, going back to their casa to dry them. Fat ones, thin ones, some were pregnant, others with babies in their arms. Some *Indio*, some part black, he was busy women-watching when three men rode in. They brushed the dust off their leather clothing, looked around warily while their horses drank. Several times they half upholstered their six-guns like men did when they were concerned about the availability of their side arms.

"I changed my mind. Draw me a beer."

"Who rode up?" the man asked in a whisper.

"Three tough hombres." He squinted through the glare and looked hard at the dust-floured riders. Not ordinary vaqueros, these men were hard cases.

"You don't know them?" he asked, drawing the beer.

Slocum took the mug and shook his head. "I'll be in the back."

"But what if they're bandits?"

"I have no gun to help you."

The man glanced sideways and then back at Slocum. "Here, it's loaded."

Slocum took the cap and ball pistol he guessed was a .44 and stuck it in his waistband. With a sharp nod, he went to a back table and sat down with his beer. He moved the gun butt some so the barrel didn't jab him. Then he held a watchful eye on the batwing doors.

The first man's spur rowels rang when he came across the flagstone porch and pushed the sombrero off on his shoulders. Entering the doors with his hands resting on top of the frame, he paused halfway through them. His eagle eyes looked around and nodded sharply at Slocum, then he went to the bar. Number two in the barroom was a gringo kid with red hair. The last one was a short, thickset Mexican. The first man motioned the two to the bar—handsome and big, he also moved with the lightning quickness of a wolf.

"Hey, gringo, what brings you here?" The redhead asked, seeing Slocum in the back.

He looked up and smiled. "All the water."

The redhead laughed at his words, raised his jigger of whiskey, saluted Slocum and downed it. He slapped the glass on the bar, dug out a coin from his vest and tossed it on the surface. "More whiskey, *mia amigo*."

The redhead acted satisfied and turned to drinking tequila with Shorty. The three conversed in low voices while Slocum nursed his beer slow-like.

"Where's the pussy?" the redhead asked the bartender.

"Two are with the soldiers."

"That's all you got?"

"This is not a busy place to afford very many."

"I want some," the redhead said. "I'm more important than them damn soldiers."

"I can do nothing—" The bartender turned up his palms and looked hopeless back at him.

"Aw, shit—Caruso," the redhead cussed. "What am I going to do?"

"Maybe you jack off." Caruso laughed, then downed another jigger. "Come on, I bet we can find you some. See you," he said to Slocum and led the way to the doors.

Caruso whistled at something or someone when he cracked the batwings to leave.

"Well, gawdamn," the redhead swore and turned to Caruso. "Who's she?"

"I don't know, but she is real pretty."

Slocum rose and sauntered over as the doors shut behind Shorty. He wanted to see what had them so impressed and he reached the batwings in time to recognize the center of their attention: it was the patron's daughter. The redhead had caught her by the arm and was drawing her to him.

"Tell him to let her go and apologize," Slocum said to Caruso.

"He's a big boy—"

"Now!" Slocum drew the .44 and shoved a door back with his body to expose the six-gun. "Hey, let go and get away from her."

The redhead whirled her around by her arm, using her as a shield, and blinked in disbelief at the sight of his gun. "You're a dumb bastard. You kill me, they'll gun you down."

"Yes, but you'll be dead."

"You might hit her. Then what?"

"Listen you little coward, let go of her or die."

"He's not fooling, Rojo," Caruso said quickly. "This hombre will shoot your eye out."

Seconds pounded like hours, then the redhead released her and grinned. "I was only fooling—hey, hey, come back here. I love you."

But despite his pleading, the girl wasted no time heading for the two-story building and without turning back disappeared in the front doorway.

"We'll be going now," Caruso said to Slocum.

Slocum nodded that he'd heard him and uncocked the pistol. He felt strange not having his own holster, so he held the gun in his hand beside his leg. The three mounted their horses. The big man saluted him and they rode out through the gates. Standing under the palm-frond porch, Slocum knew how hard the red-head seethed over him taking his prize away. Too damn bad.

"Senor! Senor!" Campos came running from the front door. "My God, you are brave. Three bad banditos and you stood them up for my daughter's honor. How can I ever repay you?"

"Nothing is necessary," Slocum said, then spun the cylinder back so the hammer would be on empty.

"But, senor. I want to do something for you."

Slocum went back inside, put the Colt on the bar.

"*Gracias*," the bartender said and stowed it away underneath.

Slocum went back to finish his beer.

"What's going on out here?" Franco emerged from the blanket-covered doorway.

"Senor Slocum saved my daughter, Juanita, from some bad banditos."

"How did he do that?" Franco asked, rubbing his neck and looking at Slocum.

"I loaned him a pistol," the bartender said. "I think he saved all of us."

"Good," Franco said and put his elbows on the bar. "Give me some whiskey."

The noncom never mentioned the matter again until they headed across the square for the house. Franco said, "I guess if you'd wanted to break out, you'd have done it when you had the gun."

"I could have."

"That Caruso is a tough hombre."

"It wasn't him. Some redheaded kid he called Rojo was the one snatched her. Caruso told him I'd kill him if he didn't release her and he believed I could."

"Was he crazy, grabbing her here on the hacienda grounds?"

"No, the kid thought this was some village and she was free goods."

"I'd sure take her if she were free," Franco mumbled as they reached the doorway.

Campos showed them in the house and poured them wine in goblets. Then they went in the dining room with the long table and high-back chairs. Slocum saw her and nodded.

"My daughter Juanita," Campos said, and she curtsied for them.

"I am so grateful to you, sir," she said and took his arm to show him where he would sit.

"I will show you," Campos said to Franco.

Slocum didn't miss seeing the envy in the sergeant's hard look at him when he turned to follow her. He let her guide him to a place on the right so he would be seated beside her. The noncom would be across from them. Campos sat at the head.

"So you leave early in the morning?" the patron asked as the women began delivering him platters of food. There were large thin slices of browned beef roast, black beans, rice cooked in tomatoes and peppers and freshly made flour tortillas.

"Ah, yes, we ride to the mountains," Franco said.

"You will find your scouts?"

"Oh, yes," Franco bragged.

Juanita put Slocum's overfilled plate before him and shared a smile, when he said softly, "That's more than I can eat."

"I doubt it," she said, looking away amused.

"But I'll sure try. Thank you," he said to his host and nodded to her.

"What do you do when you aren't helping the army, senor?" she asked, acting busy with a napkin in her lap.

"I'm a businessman."

"Married with a family, no doubt?"

"No, neither."

"Where is your home?"

"Where my business is."

"Oh," she said and raised up, shaking her raven black curly hair in a haughty manner.

He guessed her age as late teens, maybe twenty. Petite, she was no bigger than Billie. Her facial features were chiseled beauty. Sharp, but clear defined, nothing in excess—even her lips looked small. But her eyes, great pools of brown, were capped by thick lashes and sleepy lids that made his balls roil.

"The food is excellent," Franco said.

"Ah, I am so pleased you like it," Campos said.

"And, of course, your daughter is, as always, charming."

"We appreciate your soldiers visiting my hacienda. It shows such desperadoes as Caruso who my friends are," Campos said.

Slocum heard the words. So the man worries about the outlaws and hopes the *federales* presence keeps them at bay. Between bites, he considered Juanita's small hands. Tiny fingers grasped the silver fork and held the napkin when she patted her mouth.

He managed to finish his plate and she nodded smugly at him like *I-told-you-so*. Through eating, Campos invited them to smoke a cigar outside on the patio.

She asked them to excuse her and they agreed. Slocum never missed the look of envy in Franco's eyes when she swept out of the room. The girl was more than the noncom could stand not to have for himself.

They went on the patio and two men began to play guitars for their entertainment. One sang of the "Wild Cabayo." Cigars lighted, they lounged in pillow-covered chairs and listened.

After a few songs, Franco said the dawn would come early. Campos agreed and showed them to their individual rooms with a promise to have someone wake them at 3:30 AM.

"Be damn sure that you're still here in the morning," Franco said to Slocum before he went into the adjoining room.

"I could have left with them three."

"You heard me."

Slocum shook his head and closed the door. It would be a luxury to sleep in such a bed, especially since he'd had no sleep the night before. He undressed and climbed onto the great down featherbed, smiling to himself. Lying on his back, his eyelids soon fell shut.

A finger pressed to his lips silenced him when he awoke with a start. In the starlight that came in the open French doors, he recognized the curly head of hair as she gathered the oversize nightgown and climbed on the high bed

"You are surprised, no?" she whispered in a giddy voice.

"I am pleased," he said softly, making room for her beside him.

"I wanted to be with you for a little while," she said, squirming on her back to make a nest and looking at the ceiling.

"I would have been disappointed if you hadn't."

She feigned hitting him with her fist. "You never expected me to come to your bed."

"No, or I'd have shaved and bathed."

"Who cares?"

"It would have been nicer." He raised up on his elbow and looked at her in the dim light. With his free hand, he reached down and drew the gown upward. She caught his wrist and stopped him.

"You have seen many women."

"But not one of your beauty."

"Liar," she hissed

He bent over and kissed her.

"We have little time," Juanita whispered. "Soon he will be ready to go." She rolled over toward him. "Be gentle with me?"

"I promise."

In a fury, she drew the gown higher and sat up to shed it off her arms onto the floor. "There."

She fell into his arms and moved to press her small proud breasts to his chest. Nimble fingers combed through his pubic hair until she found the base of his emerging erection. Encircling it with her fingers, she drew her fist out to the head. She tore her lips from his and gasped, "My God!" when she discovered the size of his dick.

He put his finger to her lips to quiet her. No need to wake that bear Franco; he'd never appreciate her being with him in bed like this.

In an instant, she crawled over Slocum and settled on top of his muscle-corded belly and began to use his dick for a lollipop. Her tongue rasped the crown and made it stiffer and harder, until he couldn't stand it a moment longer. He pulled her off and moved to be on top of her. In seconds, he was easing his throbbing dick into her lubricated cunt. The way was tight and she spread-eagled to give him access. Soon inside the muscular ring, he began to pump her and his breath soon raged. Dizzy with passion, they strove to reach that high plateau of floating away.

Then he knew the explosion was coming. Like great needles stuck in both sides of his butt, he came and she arched her back for him. They collapsed in a pile and fell asleep in each other's arms. The knock on the door sent her into action. She fled the bed, gathering her nightgown while he gave a sleepy, "Coming." The shift bundled in her arms, she threw him a kiss and fled out the French doors into the garden.

"You coming?" Franco demanded outside the door.

"Yes. I'm dressing."

"Get your ass out here, we're leaving in twenty minutes."

"I'll be there."

"See that you are."

A hasty breakfast of scrambled eggs, spicy pork and tortillas was washed down with two hot cups of strong coffee. He shook Campos's hand, promised to return and see him again.

On his roan, Slocum reined his horse around in the starlight to head out. He was certain she watched him from an upstairs window. He threw a wave to all and trotted for the gates. Franco and his small company followed. What would they find ahead?

11

The day's hot, dusty journey turned up no sign of Franco's scouts. Franco was not pleased they'd disobeyed his orders and had gone ahead without him. That evening, they stayed with a goatherder and his wife. She butchered two goats and barbecued them for two dollars. The sullen soldiers sat around in the firelight and ate *cabrito* off the bone, tossing the leftover pieces to the waiting dogs.

One of the older ones, Corporal Morales, laughed quietly and elbowed Slocum. "See our sergeant is going to screw her, too."

"I would have seconds in her," a young private said, under his breath, taking more meat on the bone out of the kettle.

"When the sergeant finishes, you can have her," Morales said to him. Slocum laughed with them in private, then took his bedroll and went from the firelight to sleep. No doubt, Franco was fawning over the woman. She was pot-bellied, a very Indian-looking teenager, and Slocum had no desire for her first or second.

In the morning, they would be in the Madres foothills and he planned to escape from them up there. Their guard was getting lower and lower concerning him. He soon was asleep.

Predawn, a boot awakened him. The woman scrambled to feed them beans and coffee. Franco no longer kept her company; Slocum decided he'd taken his fill of her.

Slocum sat on the ground eating his beans and the young private of the night before sat nearby. "How much did she charge you?"

"My last ten centavos."

"Was she worth it?"

The boy looked at him rather whimsically. "She wasn't half bad."

The pot-bellied woman, with her small children hugging her skirts, waved good-bye to them when they rode out and smiled with her broken mouth, at least two dollars and ten cents richer.

Already hot and the sun wasn't even up. This would be their worst day on the trail. The mens' tempers were short; two soldiers had already fought over the loading of a cranky mule.

"You've been seeing their tracks," Franco said, riding up close to Slocum.

"Seen lots of tracks the past few days."

"No, you know I mean my scouts' tracks." He booted his horse to keep him trotting beside the roan.

"What about them?"

"Are we closer to catching them?"

"Some. Why?"

"How far ahead are they?"

"Maybe half a day. I can't be sure."

"I want to catch them by dark."

"You'll do our horses in." Slocum scowled at the man's order.

"I don't care. I need to catch them."

He set the roan into a lope. They'd all be ready to collapse if and when they did find them. Hot wind like a breath off a fire crossed his face. He wanted to close his eyes and be up there in the higher elevation. He needed a fairy godmother to take him instead of the tiring roan between his knees.

Late afternoon, they were off their mounts and leading them up the steep grade. The sunset flooded the western sky in coppery red as they fought to find the strength to stagger on. Franco shouted at his men and the animals to get moving when they had little desire to do more than stumble along.

Slocum had seen signs of circling vultures, higher up the mountain above them. He staggered along, stumbling on rock outcroppings in the trail. The ground ahead of him he could almost reach out and touch. Using the side of his soles to wedge his footing, he looked back and saw one of the horses fall on his side and roll downhill as Franco cursed the soldier.

On top, at last, Slocum shook his head in disbelief at how he had made it there. The roan rattled the stirrups, shaking off his weariness and then snorting in the dust. The others staggered up beside him. Even the horse who had rolled down the hill made it.

"Gawdamn, all of you are pussies!" Franco swore and then he looked at Slocum's frown. "What's wrong?"

"Might only be a dead animal up there above us, but it's damn sure attracting lots of vultures."

Franco used his hands to shield off the glare and threw his head back. "Wonder what the hell it is?"

"I have no idea."

"Mount up and ride with me while they rest."

Slocum shook his head in disbelief and remounted. Franco led the way, forced to whip his weary horse to make him go. They went through some short jack pine and zigzagged around until they reached the next level.

When they topped out, Slocum could see the birds feasting on the stripped bodies lying on the ground. They'd found his scouts. His hand instinctively went to his waist—no gun. He searched the ponderosa pines that forested the hillside for any threat. The enemy was long gone, but the skin on the back of his neck crawled thinking about them.

Franco was having a tirade, shooting at the persistent turkey vultures and cursing the Apaches at the top of his lungs and their ancestry as well. Slocum dropped off the roan, too numb to think and sat on the ground. All that hurrying and they still got there too late.

12

They buried the three bodies at dawn. Who had they been? Slocum had not heard. He suspected they were Indians, too, or at least half-bloods hired to track the escaping Apaches.

The soldiers' horses were grazing down the way in some bosque grass. He hoped that Franco would let them rest a day—but there was no telling with that hard-ass noncom. He needed the roan rested if he ever hoped to make an escape in the mountains ahead. They were vast enough to hide the whole population of Mexico, but such a plan required a sound fresh horse.

On foot, Franco had been looking for the tracks of the killers, but Slocum knew he would only find them if the Apaches wanted him to. If those three had run into a trap, it would be impossible for them not to do the same thing. If there was any way for him to avoid such a horrible death, he intented to do so.

"You ever been here before?" the private who'd screwed the goat herder's wife asked.

"Yes, but with the U.S. Army."

"They had lots of Apache scouts?"

Slocum nodded.

He looked around and then spoke softly, "Franco is crazy. What could we do against them?"

"I have no idea. But you're right. They could kill all of us."

Franco returned in thirty minutes, talked to his corporal, then strode over to Slocum.

"Where will he go from here?" he asked hands on his hips.

"Rio Blanco." Slocum swiveled on his boot toe, as he squatted under a pine.

"How far from here?"

"Two days on those horses."

"We can lead them on foot and save them." Arms folded, the noncom looked around in disgust. "You think the mine is up there?"

"I've never been to the mine. I was negotiating a trade. Gold for rifles and ammunition."

"But you've been here before?"

Slocum nodded. "With the army and Captain Crawford."

"Those stupid guards who shot him—Crawford could have got Geronimo and we wouldn't be in this shape."

"I'd bet good money Fox never killed your scouts."

"You know him good, huh?"

"He was only in Mexico to get the rest of his bunch. Then he was going up to San Carlos and doing his damnedest to avoid Geronimo."

"When did you make the gold deal?"

"In that livery where you had him prisoner."

Franco frowned at him. "They were under guard."

"Hell, them two were so busy screwing some *puta*, all those Apaches could have escaped then."

Franco laughed. "I wondered if you really got in there. I hired her to entertain those stupid donkeys. I was surprised too that they did not escape that night."

"I found the files on the forge for them while I was there."

He nodded. "Sometimes I believe you, sometimes I don't. But you were there all right. Saddle up, we lead the horses," he said to his command. "And walk."

Moans came from his men as they stiffly rose to obey. Dismounted cavalry were never happy individuals. Slocum tossed his hull on the roan. It would be a long day, he decided cinching up the girth. And Franco didn't care.

By midafternoon, they found some pot holes to water the horses and in the higher elevation, the forage looked better for the animals. Slocum's legs were stiff from climbing all the steep trails. He sat flat on his butt and tried to devise a plan to get out of the noncom's grasp. How long his charade about the gold mine would last he was uncertain. Sooner or later, Franco would expect results. He wasn't rushing up the mountain for a fistful of dry dirt.

With the roan chomping grass nearby, Slocum sat thinking about his next move. Separated from the others by 150 feet or more, he spotted some movement in the timber above them.

"Apaches!" he shouted.

His cry was answered with mushrooms of gun powder from the hillside. Two soldiers went down, hard hit. Franco was firing his revolver at them. Bullets like angry hornets filled the air. Slocum jumped in his saddle and headed for the brushy evergreens a hundred yards ahead. Riding low in the saddle, he charged the roan into the cover.

All he could hope for was that the Apaches were too busy with Franco and his patrol to pursue him. Without a gun or large knife, his chances for survival in the Madres were slim, but he at least was out of the noncom's clutches.

A check over his shoulder showed no pursuit and the gunfire was now more distant, so he faced forward again and pushed the roan harder. Any seven-year-old Apache could track his shod horse, and he needed enough space between him and them to make the effort more than it was worth.

By the time the sun died in a bloody flair in the west, he found himself resting beside a stream where he slept for the night.

By noontime, he was in the foothills and in late afternoon he found a herder of sheep and goats. An old man with snowy whiskers and hair under a dirty sombrero and tattered serape. He nodded when Slocum rode up.

"You come from the mountains?" he asked and tossed his head at them.

"Yes."

"Is it cool up there?"

"Cool at night."

"Yes."

"If I were younger I would go up there and live."

"Tough trail to get up there."

"I know it well. My son says I would only get dizzy and fall to my death if I try to go up there again."

"Your son is wise." Slocum undid the cinch to relieve the roan, who blew in the dust.

"There is water for him and beans we can share in my camp."

"I have no money."

"I saw you had no gun. Did bandits rob you?"

"Yes. I escaped with my horse and life."

The old man nodded and using the staff he leaned on, started across the hillside for a camp.

The ramada was made of gnarled barkless poles and a yellow canvas cover tied down with rawhide strips. The man's things were meager. A small sheet-iron cook stove, an iron pot and a few utensils. He served Slocum beans on a bark plate.

"You are most generous to a stranger," Slocum said, seated on an old worn blanket he spread on the sloping ground for him.

"You have no malice in your eyes. You don't covet anything I might have."

"You can see that?"

"I have been on this earth over eighty years. I've outlived three wives. I have many children and grandchildren and great-grandchildren I don't know. They say come live with me, grandfather. But they have no place for my dogs and animals."

Slocum nodded. His beans tasted good, no doubt flavored with some of the red chilies that hung overhead.

"I would die without them—my animals."

"They are the secret to your long life?"

The old man nodded. "Every day I catch a doe and drink some of her milk. Not much—" He held his crooked finger and thumb an inch apart. "But that is an elixir for me. Fresh hot milk."

"Your food was delicious."

"How long since you ate last?"

"This morning. I had three fine trout I cooked the night before."

The old man nodded as if satisfied. "You are like me, a survivor."

Slocum had not thought about it. So busy scrambling to escape Franco, surviving was what he'd done.

"I have a rifle. It is a single shot. I would loan it to you."

Slocum considered his offer. "But you may need it when the coyotes or wolves threaten your herd."

The old man shook his head. "My eyes have deep shadows in them. I could never see them unless they were close." He rose unsteady and went to a wooden crate with a hinged lid. He removed the weapon wrapped in a canvas cloth. Then he came back over, his gait unsteady. Seated on the ground, he laughed as he unwrapped it.

The fine rifle he held up to Slocum was a low-walled .25/.20 Winchester, lever action. An accurate enough gun at fifty yards that used new center-fire cartridges. The old man nodded in approval when Slocum worked the action that dropped down and ejected the shell.

"Won't your heirs want this?"

"They would only fight over it." The old man laughed. "This way they won't argue. I'll get the shells."

Slocum stopped him and set the hexagon barrel gun aside. "I can get them."

"They are in a small gray sack."

He found them. There were over three dozen, he decided and rejoined his host.

"My name is Slocum." He took his place again and began stuffing the shells in his vest pockets.

"Ramon is mine. I am glad you came by and had time for me."

"It is my good fortune to find you. You feed trail dusty strangers and give them your valuables."

"A gift that is truly appreciated is the best gift of all."

"I consider this one of the best gifts I have ever been presented. One that was never more needed either."

"I grow sleepy. I must be certain the dogs have the goats in the pen." He used his staff to rise. "They keep them there. I don't close a gate. That's so in case I die in my sleep they won't die of starvation."

"I understand and must take care of my horse," Slocum said.

"It will be good to share my camp with you."

"Yes, amigo. It will be good to sleep with a friend."

"Too bad we don't have some young women to share our blankets." The old man shook his head and started for the pen, cackling at his own words. "Ah, those were the days."

"Yes," Slocum agreed, wondering where Billie was.

He rode out after a breakfast of Ramon's reheated beans. Thanking the old man, he headed the roan northwest in a long trot, the rifle resting across his lap. Perhaps he could make the Campos Hacienda by dark. He planned to go there next.

Midday, a coyote appeared, loped along parallel to his course. Tongue out, the old sun dog was eaten up with mange and obviously in the advanced stages of the disease. Whole patches of his hide were gone, the skin crusty and raw. Slocum shut down the roan and dismounted. He used the saddle seat for a rest and drew a bead on him through the rifle's buck-horn sights.

Hammer back, he squeezed off a shot. The coyote crumbled in a heap and was on its way to a more peaceful place than his itching sore existence on earth. Slocum put a fresh cartridge in the chamber and swung up and rode over, balancing the short rifle butt on his knee. The bullet had blown the dog's heart out the far side. It sure never suffered.

Satisfied his new rifle was extremely accurate, he headed for Campos Hacienda. A picture of the grim-faced Franco entered his thoughts, as he stared across the heat wave–distorted desert ahead.

13

The quarter moon hung in the east. He rode past fields of rustling corn stalks and entered the gates in the starlight. First came an alleyway, a dark abyss, then he entered the square, which was illuminated by the lamplight escaping the cantina and the house. At the well, he dismounted and found his sea legs held him. The roan dropped his head and blew the day's dust out of his nostrils.

"Who is here?" a voice called.

"An amigo," Slocum said, undoing the girth.

"Patron, it is the one called Slocum," the voice said.

"Good," Campos shouted. "*Mi amigo*, are the others with you?"

Slocum waited as the gelding drank deep at the trough. Campos and an armed man quickly joined him.

"No, I don't know where they are. We were attacked by the Apaches and I had no gun, so I ran."

"But what happened to the sergeant and his men?"

"I'm not certain. What's wrong here?"

"Those banditos have taken my poor Juanita and I have no pistoleros to go after her."

"When?"

"Two days ago."

"Have the boy feed my horse some grain after he cools him. I need some food and you can tell me all about it."

"But you are only one man. What can you do against them?" Campos directed him to the cantina. "We can find you food and something to drink in here."

"Good." He needed a drink. At that moment, he needed lots of things. "Do you have any pistols you can spare me?"

The man looked vexed at him under the lamplight of the bar room "We have a few rifles and shotguns."

"I've got a rifle." He sat the Winchester on the tabletop and pulled out a chair. "I need a pistol or even two."

"I hate guns, so I don't have many. The *federales* are supposed to protect the citizens, so I don't hire pistoleros. This is the eighteen-eighties, we aren't supposed to have to live like cavemen."

"Cavemen kidnapped your daughter," he said, taking the whiskey bottle and glass from the bartender.

"Ramon, bring the senor that pistol you keep."

Slocum poured the whiskey in his glass and offered some to the overwrought Campos, who shook his head.

Ramon brought over the six-shooter wrapped in a bar towel and set it on the table.

"You ever shoot it?" Slocum looked up at the man holding his glass ready to taste the brown liquor.

"Once a long time ago."

"You have any ammo and caps?" He tossed down some of the sharp-tasting whiskey. It cut some of the dust in his throat.

"*Si*, some."

"We need to go out back and bust a few rounds."

Campos, the man with the rifle and Ramon agreed, and led the way out the back where the brown bottles were in a pile. Slocum cocked the hammer and they all held their ears as he fired it at the quarter moon. The second one clicked on a dud. Round three was only half a shot, four and five not as loud as the first.

"What is wrong with it?" Campos asked.

"The loads were old. Maybe the powder drew moisture. We need to boil some water. You have an extractor?" he asked Ramon.

"*Si.*"

"Boil some water. We'll clean it and reload it." He wanted to say 'and fix it,' but he was uncertain the supplies Ramon had were not unlike the ones in the gun. Old and compromised by moisture and age.

He stripped the pistol down and removed the bullet that didn't fire from the cylinder. Then he poured out the old powder in a small pan. When he looked up a buxom woman held a heaping tray of food for him.

"Wait a minute," he said, and moved things aside for her to put it down. "My, that smells wonderful."

She bowed her head. "I hope it is enough. And I go to the chapel now to pray and burn a candle that you find our lovely Juanita."

"I will find her and bring her back." His glance met the woman's and she nodded that she believed him.

"God ride with you, senor," she said, about ready to cry as she rushed out of the room.

Ramon washed the parts in the boiling water and dried them while Slocum enjoyed the mesquite-blackened strips of steak, steaming browned peppers and onions wraped in her fresh tortillas. The rice was cooked with tomatoes, meat and jalapenos. He scooped them up with a tortilla, as he watched Ramon draw patches of cloth through the barrel of the gun with a wire hook.

Slocum put down his food, took the revolver frame and examined it against the lamplight.

"The barrel is pitted, but it'll work," he said, handing it back to the man. "We need to reload it, fire it and do it all over again."

Ramon smiled. "You want to be certain it works?"

"It might be my life depends on it against them." He looked the man squarely in the eye. "Get some lard, too."

The armed guard agreed and ran off to get some at his patron's wave.

"Lard'll keep it from cross-firing," Slocum said and went back to eating the delicious food. He couldn't understand why Campos wasn't fatter eating her fare. It sure was a big relief after existing on Mexican army grub and even the old man's beans.

Once the pistol was loaded, Slocum took it outside and test-fired it. This time all five shots sounded alike and had equal force. He nodded in approval.

"Let's clean her and reload," he said, handing it to Ramon. The man nodded as if pleased the pistol had done okay.

"Where do these bandits hang out?" Slocum asked them, walking back inside with the three men.

"They say a deserted hacienda near Los Palmos," the patron said.

"Lots of them empty ones up there. The Apaches drove everyone of the entire northern half of Sonora."

"I hate to keep talking about her, but my poor Juanita, please find her and bring her back to me."

"I'll start for there in the morning. I'll need a bedroll, some cooking gear, beans, rice, salt, peppers, bacon if you have any."

"We will have it all ready for you," Campos said. "And a good mule to pack it."

"I could sure use a bath and a shave if we can squeeze it in."

"No problem. Jose, go arrange for it at my casa."

The guard nodded and hurried out the batwing doors.

Slocum looked over the traces of food left on the tray and wiped his mouth on a hand towel. "These were the same men that I had the standoff with here?"

"Ah, *si*. The one they called Rojo with the orange hair was in charge."

"Was the man Caruso with them?"

Campos looked at Ramon and then the two shrugged and turned up their hands—they didn't know. Damn, it was the work of the red head with some others.

"Your bath is ready, senor," Jose said, sticking his head in the batwing doors.

"Take the glass and the whiskey," Campos said, ready to herd him for the doorway.

He slipped the Colt in his waistband. It felt good to be armed again. Then he unloaded the rifle and tossed the shell in the air and caught it to slip the cartridge back in his vest pocket.

"Leave the rifle here. Ramon can clean and oil it and have it ready for you in the morning," Campos said.

"Thanks. I'll need a scabbard for it, too."

"And a holster for the pistol," Campos said. "We will have it all ready at sunup."

"I hate—"

Campos pushed him toward the door. "I will worry about these little things. You must go and find my daughter. Hurry, the water gets cold even as we speak."

"Thank you, Ramon, for the gun and help," Slocum said and held the whiskey bottle up by the neck as Campos hurried him for the house.

The buxom cook met him and took his hat. "What is your name?" he asked.

"Maria."

"Great food you fixed for me."

"I am glad you liked it." She waited and at last said, "I must wash and dry your clothing."

"You mean you want me to undress right here?"

"Or in the kitchen. I have seen many men. I am not afraid of seeing you."

"Fine, ma'am," he said and toed off his boots. "Heavens, I've been held up before, but never for my clothing."

Campos laughed. "Maria runs this place. I only own it."

"That's pretty clear." Slocum handed her his vest.

"I see it needs some mending." After a thorough inspection, she laid it over her arm.

He pulled his shirt off over his head and handed it to her. Then he undid the silk bandana. Galluses down, he unbuttoned the pants, thinking, *Lady, I don't wear any underwear. Oh well.*

"Socks, too," she said, taking his pants as if unimpressed by the sight of him naked.

He stood on one foot, then the other, taking them off for her.

"Your bath is in the kitchen. When you get ready to be rinsed, call me and I'll come do it for you."

He said he would and followed the shorter Campos.

"Maria is very upset over Juanita's abduction," Campos said, and they went over the smooth tile floors through the house and into the food-scented kitchen.

"You can take your bath and I will arrange for everything. Sleep in the same room as last time when you are ready to turn in."

"I can find it by myself. Oh, yeah, get me up at four AM."

"*Si*, that is early—"

"I have many miles to ride."

"You will be awakened at four. I can't tell you how—"

"You're doing your part." Slocum waved him away and took a swig out of the neck of the bottle. Maybe, after all that happened, the gun-shy little man would hire some tough pistoleros for his protection. He was damned lucky to still be alive; men like Campos who hated guns and didn't carry them, seldom lived long in Mexico.

At first, the steaming hot water shocked his body when he stepped into it and eased himself down in the high-backed copper tub. But in a short time, the tight muscles in his back began to relax and the whiskey eased him even more. He could have gone to sleep there, but instead he soaped and washed himself all over.

"Maria," he called out, not wanting to wake the dead or those lucky enough to be in bed.

She appeared in the kitchen and set down some towels on the wash-worn worktable. "You can sit in that chair when you are dry, I will shave you."

"Thanks," he said and rose for her to rinse him.

She stood on the chair and poured a wooden bucket of tepid water over him.

"Enough?" she asked. "I can get more."

His eyes shut, he reached for a towel. "That's plenty."

"Here," she said and closed his hand on the cloth.

"*Gracias.*" He began to dry himself and watched her strop a razor for his shave. When he was dry, she motioned for him to take the chair. Soon his face was hot lathered with a pig hair brush and she was busy scraping away the whiskers. No nonsense, she soon was rinsing his cheeks and around his mouth with a wet cloth.

"There you are done. I will send your clean clothes when I awaken you."

"A bed about now sounds wonderful. *Gracias.*" He used the towel to wrap around his waist and set out for the bedroom down the hallway.

"Senor, find my girl," she said softly.

He paused and looked back. "You're her mother?"

She shook her head, standing in the lighted doorway. "No, her mother died giving her life. I am the one that raised her."

"You did a fine job." He nodded and went on.

In the predawn, Campos sat across from him at a table. "I am giving you some money in case you need it. If they want a ransom I will pay it for her unharmed return."

Slocum nodded he heard the offer and glanced at the buckskin pouch full of money. As he finished his burrito of salsa, eggs and ham, Slocum considered Campos's words. *Unharmed.* He doubted that Juanita was unharmed by this time in the hands of the horny, redheaded kid. To get her back would be a big enough job—unscathed impossible.

"My man Jose can ride with you."

"You need him here. Besides I must sneak in close to get her out. One man is enough."

"As you say, but I wish that Sergeant Franco and his men were here to go with you."

"I'll be fine."

"God help you, *amigo*."

Slocum left on the refreshed, well-rested roan leading a good-size pack mule that needed no encouragement to keep up. With a small rifle across his lap, he saluted the hacienda help that had gathered as well-wishers. In a long trot, he swung out of the gate across the small irrigation ditch bridge and headed for the low line of saw-tooth hills in the soft light of dawn.

People always knew who rode past them. A small bribe to a woman and she could describe them right down to the clothes they wore. For a drink in a cantina, a vaquero would know if one of their horses had a limp by the tracks in the dust. No one in Sonora was deaf, dumb or blind at the same time. A blind beggar in Altus Regale had once told him a man with silver spur rowels had gone by his spot only minutes before—a gunfighter who'd killed one of Slocum's friends, Adriano Valdez. In a short while, Slocum had found the man and sent him to hell, too.

A redheaded kid in Sonora wouldn't be hard to find. By late afternoon, he came across a herder who shared some frijoles around a fire and told him about the passage of the redhead, Juanita and the others. The herder and Slocum squatted at his small fire and ate the reheated beans.

"She was a princess." The man shook his gray-bearded face as if disappointed with her plight. "He was leading her on a big bay horse. I could see the pain in her eyes, even at a distance."

"How many rode with him?"

"Three, one was short and broad like a toad in the saddle. The other two were vaqueros and they all rode behind looking back all the time like the devil was on their tracks."

"He was," Slocum said.

"They are tough hombres. Even the vaqueros."

Slocum nodded that he understood the herder's warning. He dug out two pesos from his vest pocket and handed them to the man. "For my food and the words I needed to know."

"You are far too generous, *mi amigo*."

"No, you are a poor man of goats and sheep. Her father who cries for her return is very rich and he wants to thank you for your help with a little money."

"More money than I ever see."

"Smoke a good cigar, maybe find a young *puta* and a good bottle of wine."

The man, as if deep in his own thoughts, agreed with a gentle bob of his head. "Ah, that would be heavenly."

"I need a few hours sleep," Slocum said. "So I will be gone when you awaken."

"God be with you, *mi amigo*."

"*Gracias*." He went off to put a feed bag on his animals, then sleep those precious few hours.

When he awoke, the heat had evaporated from the desert. Under a spray of stars, Slocum tightened the cinches and prepared to ride on. Still groggy from his limited slumber, he swung in the saddle and rode north. The trail wasn't that cold; he'd find them.

He met the sun's rise over the horizon on his right. Riding through the tall cacti and greasewood, he looked for a line of cottonwoods. The town of Cabeza was a few miles ahead, actually more a gathering of hovels rather than a town. Someone there would tell him the truth about their passage. A woman he knew named Lupe lived there—he recalled her. Maybe if she was still there, she could tell him.

Riding into the village, he drew suspicious looks from dark-eyed children who stopped playing to observe his passage. Some women gathered their little ones to their skirts like hens did chicks to protect them from the shadow of a hawk. He heard their sharp commands. "Come here! Now!"

He stopped before a jacal and called out, "Lupe?"

A woman in her thirties came out. Gray streaked her hair and she swept it back using her hand to shield the sun's glare to look up at him.

"Ah, Slocum," she said, recognizing him. She smiled big.

"You still live here?" he asked with a grin, dismounting heavily.

"What else can I do? I have no money to leave."

"Poor Lupe, midwife and doctor and *bruja*."

She shook her head in disapproval at his word for a witch.

"Shush, you will hurt my business calling me that. Who wants a witch to deliver their newborn?"

"We can see to the animals later," she said as he undid the latigoes on the roan. "When did you eat last?" Her arm linked in his elbow, she pulled him toward the doorway.

"Let me relieve this mule a little and I will be ready to visit."

She let go, swept the wave of hair back, standing close and looking up at him as he tended to the mule. "You eaten anything in the last few days?" she asked again when he was done.

He turned around, took her in his arms and kissed her hard on the mouth. When he let her go, she smiled with a knowing look, locked her elbow over his arm again and took him into the house. "Come, I have some food and we can talk."

A last check of the village showed nothing out of place that concerned him and he went after her through the doorway. She showed him a worn blanket to sit upon and went to the fireplace for his food.

She returned with a tray of beans and rice in a thick tomato sauce and pulled meat. He nodded in approval and she set it before him, then made another trip across the room. Corn tortillas on a tray and red wine she poured from a bottle in a mug for him. Then she knelt beside him and hugged his shoulder. Laying her cheek against his arm, she finally released him to eat.

"I am so happy you came to see me," she said and settled sitting cross-legged beside him.

He acknowledged her pleasure with a nod. "An outlaw kidnapped a rich man's daughter. He came this way. He was redheaded and three vaqueros rode with him."

Busy filling his tortilla, he glanced at her. "You see them?"

"You'd better forget them." Her brown eyes showed her deep concern over the matter.

"Why?" he asked, busy completing the construction of his rollup. Sampling some of the fire-braised meat, he looked at her hard. What was wrong? A *bruja* knew things others did not in this land.

"I see things that are very bad for you."

"They've passed through here?" Ignoring her warning, he cocked an eyebrow at her and listened for her reply.

"Yes, two days ago. But you should not go any farther on this business." She sat back, hugged her knees and shook her head warily.

"You mean there's real danger in it for me?"

"Oh, *si*. Much danger." The frown on her smooth forehead showed her worry.

"Well—" He leaned over and kissed her. "I'd better get on my armor. I told the man I would try to recover his daughter."

"These men you go after are very cruel."

He agreed with her assessment between bites of her tasty food.

"No way that I can make you stay here with me and not go after them?"

"Lupe, my love, nothing would make me happier, but I owe some allegiance to the girl as well."

"I see. When you leave, I will burn candles in the chapel for you. Now," she said getting up. "I will unload your mule and horse. I have some hay."

"I can do—" he started to protest.

"No, you rest and eat. I want every ounce of energy you have left for myself."

"Do I look that weak?"

"No, but I want you very powerful for me." She laughed, going out the front door.

Slocum thought he heard a sole on the gritty gravel behind his back. He tossed the food aside and threw himself to the side. The shot filled the room with blinding sulfurous gun smoke. Slocum thumbed back the hammer on his cap and ball pistol and took aim at the shape in the doorway. His gun responded with an ear-shattering blast. The vaquero with the smoking gun began to crumble—shot in the heart, his knees buckled and his gun hand went limp at his side. He dropped his revolver and then fell facedown.

Slocum scrambled past his body and made it to the door. He could see Lupe struggling with another man dressed similar to the first. When the second vaquero saw Slocum emerging, he shoved her aside, took a quick shot and splintered the door frame. That gave Slocum the time to answer him. The bullet struck the gunman in the chest, spinning him halfway around. Standing for moment, he looked like a broken-necked chicken. The sombrero bobbed forward on his head, then his knees buckled and he fell to the ground like a toppled tree.

Fingers pressed over her mouth, Lupe screamed from behind her hand. Brown eyes wide open in shock, she stared in disbelief as the gunman crumbled in a pile at her feet. Slocum was at her side in a second.

"See any more of them?" he asked, out of breath.

"No. Who are they?"

"My guess is they work for Rojo." Satisfied that there was no sign of any more gunmen, he spun the cylinder around to the last spent chamber and dropped the hammer. The .44 holstered, he knelt down and spoke to the man on the ground.

"What is your name?"

"Raul—"

"You work for Rojo?"

The man made a slight nod. His face contorted with pain. His right hand that he held over the wound seeped red blood.

"You tell me where he is and I'll see you have a Christian burial."

"*Si*, senor—" he managed. "He is at the Stone Ranchero. . . ." The man closed his eyes, grimaced, then jerk-kicked his spur-clad boots in death's final throes. His rowels rang like church bells.

"How many more ride with Rojo?" Slocum asked her.

She shook her head and ducked into his hug. "They are mean men who value nothing, but money. So many are out of work. You can hire a vaquero, a pistolero for ten pesos a month."

"The Apaches forcing so many to flee, huh?"

"All the ranches in northern Sonora and Chihuahua are empty, because of those red devils."

"But this Stone Ranch?"

"It is a fortress. No one can get in it. But they could not raise cattle, so they went to Mexico City and pray that the U.S. soldiers and scouts will get them out."

"He just move in it?"

"*Si*." She swept her hair back and smiled at him as if part of her upset over the shooting had fled once she'd been held in his arms. "Who is there to stop him? No one."

"So I can't storm the gates and get in, huh?"

"You can't get within half a kilometer of that place."

"Many guards?"

"Many and they have telescopes and the land has all been swept bare up to this place."

"How far away?"

"A day's ride northwest of here."

"I want to go see it."

"You are crazy." She frowned at him in disapproval.

"Maybe, but I must try and get her from them. Who will take these bodies away and have them buried?"

"For ten pesos, they will give them a church burial."

He dug in his vest and gave her the money. "Find them and I will finish my supper."

"What about the one inside?" She gave a head toss that way.

"I'll drag him outside for the undertaker."

"What about any money on them?"

"Yours, they owe me. And their guns, I want them; they're better than mine."

"Can I have this one's concho belt?"

"Finders, keepers," he said. "They won't need anything where they're going."

"Good, they can go to hell in their underwear," she said, as she bent over and pulled off a boot.

He dragged the dead one in the doorway outside. She practically had the the first one down to his long handles. She looked up and smiled at him. "This one had a good hunting knife. I can use it."

"Good."

"Sorry, your food is cold," she said and bundled up everything in her arms.

"I'm just glad I'm here to eat it." He laughed and went back to make himself another rollup. While he sat on the blanket and chewed his food, she came in out of breath with the second one's outfit.

"I must go find Pedro and his son."

"Good enough, I won't leave."

She moped her sweaty face on a cloth and smiled. "You'd better not." Then, with a swirl of her pleated skirt, she was gone.

14

The sun burned out in a final red burst beyond a saw-toothed range in the distance. Night insects began to sizzle. Pedro had hauled away the bodies, promising a prayer would be said over each one as they were buried and that when the priest made his monthly visit he would say the last rites over them. That cost two dollars more. Slocum paid the man and thanked him.

With a yoke over her shoulders, Lupe brought back two wooden pails of water from the community well and set them down on the floor of the room. "So we can clean up some."

"Good idea."

In minutes, she lit two small candles for light that made her shadow on the wall look like a giant's. She undid the strings holding her blouse closed and then smiled at him.

"You still enjoy watching me undress?" she paused and waited for him to speak.

"Go ahead. I want an eyeful of you."

Prodded by his words, she finished unlacing her shirt and bared her proud breasts in the flickering light. They shook with their firmness and the large brown rosette nipples were pointed. Yes, this was the Lupe he recalled. With a sly grin, she undid the ties at her waist and stepped out of her skirt. The exaggerated outline of her boobs danced on the wall as she set the skirt on a bench.

He went through her ring of fire and she gave a cry. He looked down, straining to drive deeper with each stroke and saw her mouth was open, gasping in pleasure. Eyes half-closed, she

115

looked intoxicated by the forces plying her body. His body responded as the ring grew tighter. She locked her legs around him and raised her butt up until their pelvis bones were rubbing against the coarse pubic hair between them.

Air became a precious commodity, as their breath roared through their throats. She clung to him in the whirling dance that powered them deeper and deeper into the arms of passion's fire. Then he felt a lightning bolt in his left nut and knew the end was near. He wanted to be the deepest he could get when the cannon fired. He strained against her and the red hot cum flew out the end of his dick in rocket fashion.

She fainted.

His arms stiffened to hold his weight off of her. He smiled in the candlelight at the drunken *bruja. My, my, what a lady.* He closed his eyes and withdrew his sword. She rested on her back, waving her arms over her head in snakelike fashion when he moved over beside her.

"Mother of God, I could do that every night if you stayed here."

A hard nipple scratched his palm as he idly fondled it. Slocum smiled at her words, then shook his head. "They'd only come and find me here."

"They are bastards," she swore and shook her head in disapproval. Forced to reset the hair in her face, she ran her fingers through it.

"I agree. The world is full of them. I'd better get some sleep. I want to see the fortress tomorrow."

She scooted her bare skin against him and he threw an arm over her. In minutes, he was fast asleep.

A quick hard kiss and he was off in the predawn coolness. Small clouds from the far off Gulf of California dotted the sky. Even with his hat on to shade his head, the reflected light off the ground forced him to squint his eyes at the corners to try and see farther across the rolling desert for anything or anyone that might be a threat.

At a strange sound, he drew back into the mesquite and a wash which he hoped covered his presence. The sound was a trumpet and whoever played it was coming from the east. The musician was hidden under a large straw sombrero on a small gray donkey and he tooted away on some tune as he rode. Slocum figured this one could tell him all about the fortress—if he didn't run back and tell Rojo he was out there spying on him. It was a chance he would have to take.

"Hold up!" he shouted to the musician.

The man whipped back his wide-brimmed hat and blinked in disbelief at Slocum.

"What—what do you want, senor?"

"Some information." Slocum walked out in the road leading his horse.

The man looked relieved and slumped in his saddle as if he relaxed seeing that Slocum was not any threat.

"I thought you were a bandito and wanted to steal my horn."

"No, I want to know about the ranch you came from."

"Oh—" He looked back that way and checked his small burro, which wanted to twist around. "That is bad place. Those men are mean and perverts."

"How many men?"

"Oh . . ." He screwed up his full face as if counting them in his mind. "Six or eight—some are gone somewhere. They have not come back."

"Those men that are gone, did one wear a concho belt?"

"Ah, *si*, Diaz, he was a mean one, too. You see him?"

"Yesterday, so there are six left?"

"Ah, maybe four is all. Rojo makes five men and the pretty lady."

"The lady?"

"Yes, Juanita, they call her. She is the most beautiful woman in all of Mexico. Rojo, he kidnapped her somewhere. Such a shame."

"She is all right?"

He shrugged his shoulders, then shook his head. "How can she live with such an outlaw and be all right?"

"Why did you leave?"

"Ah, senor, those men are perverts and would rather corn-hole me than find a woman. They learned how in prison, they say, and like it better than the ugly *Indios* women up here."

"You ain't going back?"

The man squirmed uncomfortable in the saddle as if reliving his bad experiences. "No."

"Tell me, do they guard the walls at night?"

"No, they usually get drunk and then do their thing to whoever they can hold on to." He shook his head. "Not me anymore, thank God."

"Good to know," Slocum said and gave him a few coins.

The man nodded in appreciation, then looked him straight

in the eye. "You are going to try to get the woman out?"

"I am going to try."

"May the Virgin Mary look after you. They are mean men. Rojo, especially."

"Where does he keep her?"

"Oh, she is free. But there is no way for her to escape. She knows that now."

"Obviously she's tried."

"Yes and been whipped for her troubles. Rojo calls her his slave and believe me, she is."

"What is your name?"

"Manuel."

"Slocum and *gracias* to you. Have a safe journey."

"God be with you, too."

"I'll need him to be," Slocum said and put the reins over the roan's head. His mind was churning over all he knew. There might be a way to slip inside while they had their "fun." She was loose, but also his slave. Damn, he needed her out of there. He stepped in the saddle, listening to the horn player's music as he rode out of earshot. Stone Ranch was next.

In an hour, he was belly down on a hillside looking at the ranch's gray rock walls. They had burned a complete circle around the fortress. There would be no sneaking up on that place in the daylight. A guard in the northwest turret could see two sides. And no doubt there was another opposite him on the other side. The great gates were closed and Rojo was king of the place. Damn, how would he ever get her out?

On his belly, he eased back, satisfied there was nothing he could do until past sundown. Once out of sight, he headed down the slope on his boot heels towards the roan. All he needed was to find a secure place where the roan could graze and he could sleep a few hours. The gelding raised his head up and watched his approach.

Maybe back in these hills, he could find a resting place.

He hobbled the roan and unfurled a blanket in the shade. Hat over his face, he soon fell asleep in the lacy shade.

Something woke him. His fingers closed on the gun butt. He peeked with his right eye and saw nothing. His ears strained for even a sound—only the wind. What had awoken him? Then he heard them again.

Gunshots. Must be happening over at the ranch; he was over a quarter mile from the fortress. On his feet, he saw the roan was looking that way, too. With his field glasses in hand, he scrambled up the hillside, dodging prickly pear beds and other thorny plants to reach the summit where he crawled out and could see the turret. No one was up there standing guard when he focused the glasses. The gate was shut.

Was the fight internal or target practice? He watched the gate open. The redhead emerged leading a reluctant sorrel with Juanita aboard. Then he shot back at the gate and struck some vaquero chasing him. The man fell down hit hard.

Where in the hell was Rojo going and what had happened? He needed to get to the roan and follow him. He edged back, not near as careful as the last time, and rushed downhill. Dodging cacti and jumping a downed tree, he reached the meadow and on the run bent over to snatch the blanket up. In the corner of his eye he saw the sidewinder's diamond-like pattern in a blur as it struck at him.

The needle teeth pinpricked his arm though his shirt and he fell on his butt grasping his forearm. The serpent's triangular head raised up, his split tongue sensing for him. Slocum quickly moved away, opened the cuff and saw the two tiny marks dotted with blood. It had made its mark all right.

He used the kerchief from his neck to make a tourniquet using his teeth and left hand to pull it tight—but it would need more than that. A cut to send the poisoned blood out and not to his heart. With his left hand, he drew the razor sharp knife from his right boot and wedged it between his knees. At that angle he'd need to make two cuts so the bite marks would bleed freely.

The sidewinder still coiled a few feet away, distracting him. The snake acted as if he wasn't done with Slocum. Unusual behavior for one of that species, which usually went on their swirling way to escape man. This one still hissed and tested the air with his split tongue as if looking for the meal he expected to be numbed by this time from his strike.

It was a difficult task to make the cuts. Blood soon seeped from the wound and he let the knife drop. Then, forcing his arm around to his mouth, he sucked on the incisions and spat his own blood sideways. The arm burned like it was on fire. Damn, what luck. Rojo gone off. God knew where he went with the girl and he was a long night's ride from the only doctor in the country he knew—*Lupe*.

Still have to make the kerchief tighter—somehow, he thought.

15

"What happened to you?" she asked, rushing out in the night from her jacal.

"A snake—" he said and started out of the saddle.

She caught him and got under his arm. He felt lightheaded as if his legs were made of willow sticks as she propelled him into the room and eased him down on her bed.

"What did you do to it?"

"Cut it and sucked all I could."

"I see." She gathered her skirt to get up. "I must go get a chicken."

"I ain't hungry—" he mumbled and fainted.

When he awoke, he saw she had a cut a chicken in two to plaster on his wound and was holding it tightly in place.

"Ah, you are awake. Good, this chicken will draw out the poison."

The sharp ammonia smell, and wet feathers as well, filled his nose. Thank God he was at Lupe's place. Coming from the Stone Ranch, he wanted to pitch out of the saddle and sleep where he fell, even in a prickly pear patch.

"Drink this." She raised him up, using her knee to hold him and forced a cup of steaming tea to his lips.

"Whew," he said afterward. "Hot stuff."

"Willow bark tea, it will ease the pain. The chicken would have been better hours ago."

"Sorry, I was up there." Then he told her his story of something waking him up, then the shooting and coming back to find the source of what woke him in the first place.

"Where can he go with her?" She frowned at him concerned.

"That's the trouble, I don't know."

"Nothing is a secret in Mexico for long." She eased him back down on the pallet. "The tea will help."

His arm had swollen on the ride to her place until he feared it might burst open. But the split chicken she'd applied must have helped draw out the poison. He wasn't certain. His arm hurt and he worked it to drive out the stiffness. Thoughts of it being disabled knifed his mind. That was his gun hand and he couldn't hit a bull in the ass with his left one. In a half hour, her painkiller set in and the sharpness was dulled when he moved his limb. He fell asleep.

It was dark when he awoke. She was getting him up. Pulling on his boots for him.

"What's wrong?"

"Hush, there is someone here asking about you," she hissed in his ear. "Now get up,"

"But, they'll find my horse and mule—"

"No, I hid them earlier. Come I have a deserted jacal you can hide in." She wadded up a blanket and shoved him through the door.

"Who is it?"

"*Federales.*" She led him around some hovels and into a draw under the stars. Then she shoved him under a fallen-down jacal. "Get under there."

Crawling wasn't easy with his sore arm and she tossed in the blanket, squatting at the entrance. "I will check on you later. Be quiet down here." When he turned in his cramped quarters and looked out from under the collapsed roof, he watched her shadowy figure sweeping their tracks with greasewood branches. Then she evaporated into the night.

On all fours, he felt something crawling across his left hand. His first impulse was to strike at it. Then in the dim light he saw the outline of the intruder. Wiggling like a snake the lightning stinger tail of the scorpion was evident. He held his breath. Seconds pounded by. One move, one action would be met by the pain-filled stinger of desert legend.

He knew of cowboys who woke up and pulled on a boot with one inside. They didn't wear a boot for days on their swollen foot. He didn't need to get stung on top of the rest of his problems. At last, the scorpion left his hand and, he hoped, the area. But the creatures were like birds; they congregated. That one was not the only one in this fallen-down jacal—he must share the night with them and until the *federales* left the village. Perhaps hundreds of them were in the old ceiling made of mud and sticks only inches above him. Damn.

Searching soldiers cursed in the night going past his hideout.

"—Baca is crazy. That gringo is long gone. No way he could have killed Sergeant Franco and all those men—"

"He is the only one that is alive. Franco never returned—"

"Senor Campos said he had only a small rifle when he came to his hacienda. No pistol."

"Ah, *si*, but that could be a cover-up." Sounds of the two men pissing not five feet from his hideout made him wish he had taken along the later model Colt .44 taken from the dead vaquero he carried to replace the old cap and ball.

"I wish I could stick my dick in the patron's daughter like that Rojo is doing right now."

"Maybe she will be so grateful when we find her that she fucks all of us."

"Oh, sure. Come on, Juan, he isn't out here and I want some sleep. They say we must ride to this Stone Ranch tomorrow."

"How far is that?"

"A long damn way—" Then they were gone.

Captain DeBaca must have first gone to Campos looking for what happened to Franco. Then he took up Slocum's trail. Something else dropped on Slocum's back, then scurried off. He clenched his teeth. Another damn scorpion? It would be a long night.

Before dawn, he heard the soldiers breaking camp. They cussed the mules and horses. They cussed the ugly *putas* in their lives. And they cussed the army, then they fell into formation and rode away.

In a short while, Lupe came, bent over and hissed at him to come out.

"How did you sleep?" she asked.

"Not well. I shared that place with ten thousand scorpions."

"Oh, my—" She hugged him tight. "I never thought about them."

"I did. All night long they kept falling on me." Busy brushing himself off, he made a cloud of dust, then at last gave up.

"Did they sting you?"

"No, but they crawled all over me."

She gave a shudder, hugging his arm and taking him to her place.

"Did the *federales* hurt anyone?"

She wrinkled her nose. "DeBaca picked a young girl, Marcia, to entertain him."

"He rape her?"

"No, but he made her dance naked while he watched and drank, but when the time came, he could not get it hard enough to stuff it in her."

"Any more trouble from them?"

"They ate Jeyiffee's pig and screwed his wife, but she don't care, except she cried over them eating her fat pig."

"Did they question you?"

"*Si*," she shrugged. "I told them you went on to the Stone Ranch after you shot those vaqueros."

"He asked when I was coming back?"

"Yes. I said I didn't know. You went to find the patron's daughter."

"That's all."

"When I came out of the jacal that DeBaca was in, some corporal caught me outside and felt my breasts."

"What did you do?"

"I told him he could have himself a real bad case of the clap messing with me."

"Scared him?"

"He never came to get his clap." She laughed.

"I need to get to looking for Rojo and Juanita."

She clutched his left arm tighter. "The *federales* will find them."

"I told her father I'd find her. He paid me for that job."

She herded him across the palm-frond-covered porch and into her hut. "Breakfast is ready. Flour tortillas, scrambled eggs, chili verde and some mesquite-smoked pork the *federales* did not eat last night."

"How much was his pig worth?"

"Ten pesos, maybe less."

"Find my vest, I have that much I can pay him, since I caused them to come here."

"Jeyiffee will praise you and Lolleta will probably screw you to death."

He shook his head warily. "I don't need her."

She turned his still sore arm up to look at it. "Healing," she said and released it.

"Lots better, thanks to you." He sat cross-legged and took another bite from the tasty burrito.

She undid her blouse and then her skirt with a wicked wink at him, before she got busy taking a sponge bath in full view.

"That what's for dessert?" he asked and raised his eyebrows as if impressed.

She ran her hands down the sleek sides of her body and ended with her fingers spread out beside her tawny thighs and pushed in her shoulders. The pointed breasts quaked and she laughed when she held them up higher. "I have been called many things by men in my life, but never *dessert*."

Hours later, Slocum was sound asleep. He awoke, smelling the acrid traces of gunpowder and feeling the muzzle against his ear.

"One word, hombre, and you're dead."

Slocum froze. His heart stopped, too. He could hear Lupe struggling with others.

"So you are looking for the Senorita Campos, huh?" It was Franco's taunting voice in his ear. Someone else in the dark room was busy tying his hands behind his back. They hurt his sore arm in the process.

"Let her go, she had nothing—" The muzzle of the pistol jammed in his ear cut off his words.

"My men are going to fuck her raw. Then cut her throat. You won't be able to hide here again. Maybe not hide anywhere when I get through with you."

"Turn her loose, gawdamn it!"

"I never back up on my word to my men. You know what those fucking Apaches did to me?"

"No—" He didn't give a damn. It was the muffled sounds of Lupe straining to fight off her attackers that bothered him more.

"They hung me by my feet and tried to cook my brains."

Damn shame they didn't succeed.

"Two of my men broke into their camp and even wounded they drove them off and saved me. The same ones who are fucking your friend now." His raucous laughter rocked the night.

"They say that DeBaca has gone to the Stone Ranch to find Juanita. But you must have been there already?"

Slocum never offered to answer.

"You will beg to tell me where that Rojo took her after a day trailing my horse. If she had been at that ranch that you would have stayed there. Right?"

Slocum barely heard Franco's words, as he watched Lupe facedown on the pallet only a foot away from her second raper, who was grunting like a boar hog on top of her. He wanted to kill them all for what they were doing to Lupe. The stiff boot driven into his ribs made him cough. *Beat me, even kill me, you pig, I ain't telling you shit.* His remaining days on this earth would be pain-filled, but no difference; he was not giving this sumbitch any satisfaction. If he could only help Lupe. That brought him close to tears, his concern over her—they couldn't make him cry any other way.

Jerked to his feet by rough hands, he looked his adversary. "My boots—"

"No. They are Uvalde's now. You don't want to die with your boots on. What would your mama think if you did that?"

"I'd better never get loose," Slocum said as they drove him outside. They put a reata around his neck, threw it over the beam in front of the porch that held the palm fronds and drew him to his full height by tugging on the rope. Then they tied it off.

The short one went by and jabbed a thumb in his gut. "It is our turn to screw that sister in there next."

Slocum saved his breath and venom until his hands were free.

16

"Bet you learn to lead today," Franco bragged as he wrapped the reata around his saddle horn and booted his horse to leave. Before the slack was out of the rope around Slocum's neck and with his hands tied behind his back, he hurried to keep up to his captor. Rocks and stickers jabbed his bare soles—if he fell down, he'd be dragged to death.

Lupe was dead. They'd forced him to watch Franco kill her. Two of the cowards held her by the arms. He would never forget the horror in her brown eyes as the butcher in his filthy green uniform stepped in behind her and grasped a fistful of her long hair. Ruthlessly, he jerked her head back to expose the cords of her coffee-colored throat, then he'd laid the blade on it. Swish and blood flew all over.

Slocum pulled and fell to his knees.

Someone pulled his head up and laughed in his ear. "That bitch can fuck the devil next. He's going to get fifths."

His words drew much laughter.

Unable to wipe his sour-tasting mouth or blow his running nose, Slocum tried to stare holes into eternity across the jacal at the far wall. He'd get them all if he lived—every last one of the bastards. But Franco would die slow.

Being forced outside as they prepared to leave, he saw all the people lined up in the growing light.

"In there is the evidence," Franco pointed at the door of her jacal behind him. "That is what I do to the peons that hide criminals in this land. You don't want to ever hide one from the *federales* or you will die the same as she did."

Then the noncom swung in the saddle and Slocum's trot-to-his-death began. He'd heard them earlier speak that Franco knew something about a place on the San Pedro near the village of Arispe where Rojo might go. Like a tethered dog, hatless, Slocum's bare head exposed to the sun's burning rays, he trotted after the spent horse. Sharp rocks turned under his bare soles cutting his feet as he hurried to keep up. The spiny needles of the cholla stuck in them like a pin cushion. His only hope to survive was the poor condition of Franco's and the others' horses. Franco's mount stumbled often and blew his nose in the dust. Thank God, they'd never found his roan or even the pack mule.

Repeatedly throughout the day, Franco cussed the weary horse, but neither foul words nor his spurs would revive his strength. Before nightfall, Slocum judged the horse would drop to his knees and it would be all over. He would lie down and die. None of the others rode animals in much better shape. They would all be ridden to death. Besides Franco's weight was wearing on the horse, too. He was a big man compared to his troopers. No difference, these once-stout horses were on their last legs and it would be hard to find remounts. The greatest horse thieves of all, the Apaches, had stolen all the ones in this land that they could ride and eaten the ones they could not use.

Three hours north of the village, Franco gave the order to dismount. Slocum dropped to his knees and drew in needed gulps of air. Grateful to be off his fiery feet, he heard a familiar distressing sound from one of the soldier's mounts—a death grunt. The dust-floured bay fell over as a *federale* named Perona stepped off of him. Sprawled on the ground, its throat gurgled. The corporal named Hernandez hurried over to try and help remove his saddle and gear. In the end, three others had to help him get it off. They piled it on a second horse and then they sprawled on the ground to rest.

"Lead them," Franco said after a short while, and Slocum was barely able to stand before the noncom began to step out with the lead rope thrown over his shoulder headed for the saw-edged mountains in the north. Perona led the sergeant's horse. But the *federales* soon learned the weakened horses led slower afoot than when they'd been urging them with spurs and whips from the saddle. Their situation would have been laughable for Slocum, except for the part about Lupe's murder and his abused feet.

At nightfall they made a dry camp in a deserted ranch and gave Slocum one short hot drink from a canteen. He noticed the horses were too tired to graze. Without any water—the dug well had collapsed—the troopers could only wipe their horses' nostrils clean and wet their lips with rationed canteen water on rags. The seriousness of the men's own situation and no doubt their thoughts about being without mounts in the middle of the Sonora Desert made them silent.

"Midnight, we move out," Franco said. The bloody light of sundown shone on his unshaven face and thick lips. "We'll leave the horses and find more ahead. They will only slow us down. This way we can rest in hot afternoon."

"How far to water?" someone asked.

"I imagine a short ways and your worries will be less," Franco said.

"The only water is at San Markos," a trooper named Tomas said.

"We aren't going there!" Franco shouted. "We must go to Arispe."

"What if we are all dead?"

Franco swept off his hat and showed the scabby top of his bare skull where the hair had been burned off of it by the Apaches' fire. "I didn't endure this not to find that girl. I will marry her."

"What about Captain DeBaca?"

"Apaches will kill him." Franco chuckled. "Who will miss that bastard? He was too much of a coward to go in the Sierra Madres. Why worry about him?"

"He will court-martial you."

"Dead, he won't even fart in his grave." His words drew much laughter.

Slocum sat on the ground. Franco would never be safe as long as any of these men who knew his plans and then helped him carry them out were left alive. They, too, needed to realize he'd kill all of them to reach his own goal of having Juanita Campos for his bride.

Why was he still alive? Slocum had asked himself that question many times during the grueling day. Franco had a motive for keeping him alive, but Slocum had no idea what it was.

Out of all the confusion of the day, he tried to focus his mind on something else. Would DeBaca come back from the Stone Ranch empty-handed and track them down? No telling. He knew one thing: neither horses nor men were important to Franco; wanted one thing: Juanita.

Slocum listened to the night insects. He'd been in messes before, but this might be the worse one. No one who could come to his aid even knew where he was—or the severity of his situation.

"Get your ass up, gringo. Your beauty sleep is over, and you don't look no prettier." Franco's laughter shattered the night.

No one else laughed. They groaned and got up. In a few minutes, they struck east under the stars. His captor led him by the rope around his neck. With his hands still tied in front, he had better balance and the snake-bitten arm was not as uncomfortable. His soles and feet felt numb, as if they were not a part of his body. These lunatics had to pay for what they'd done to him and Lupe—no one else could do anything about it.

Walking along the rim, the ground gave at once and Franco fell off the bank into the dry wash. He never let go of the rope. Slocum came off the bank on the end of the reata and did a cartwheel in the air. Sprawled on his back in the sand, he blinked at the stars. Maybe he was in hell and not really on earth.

"Come on," Franco said and Slocum scrambled to get up or he'd be chocked to death. But even in the pearly light, he could see the fall had injured the big man's right leg.

"You all right?" Corporal Hernandez shouted from above them.

"Of course, I'm all right, you idiot. Apaches can't kill me; by gawd, a little fall won't hurt me." Franco gave a laugh that shattered the night. "I'll catch you up ahead. Watch out for that bank that caved off on me."

Slocum could see Franco's outline in the pearly light; he was still favoring his right leg.

17

Dawn came like a purple velvet light across the desert.

Franco's men trudged along not like a company of military men, but like a small company of drunks, inebriated on a lack of sleep, water and food. Slocum heard snippets of their prayers: "Hail Mary, mother of God . . ." ". . . glory be to the father."

Limping after the noncom, Slocum was unsure how he kept walking on the planks he called his feet. Franco stopped and rubbed his right leg. Then he threw the rope in Slocum's face. "I'm tired of pulling on your dumb ass, but I ain't too tired to pull the trigger. You try anything I'll blow your ass off."

Slocum nodded and held his hands out. "Cut the damn rope."

Franco settled back on his heels and looked hard at him. "All right, but no tricks."

Rubbing his sore wrists and flexing his arms, Slocum set out again following the limping Franco, and the men came behind him, coughing and occasionally moaning. Protests from Franco's soldiers fell on deaf ears, so they continued to pray in low mumbling voices cut hoarse by the acrid dust that boiled up in the hot wind.

No water, no appetite, slugging along in an overheated oven under the unrelenting sun and no sign of any more than a occasional lizard darting across their path for the shade of another greasewood bush. Tongues swollen from a lack of moisture and riding boots falling apart from abrasive wear on the sharp rocks. The boots had never been designed for this kind of walking and they quickly disintegrated under the harsh conditions, so soon the men were no better off than Slocum.

With no hat to shield his eyes or head, he felt dizzy looking at the desert. Rising heat waves further distorted his vision. If Franco had a plan, he wasn't telling them. His bully ways had carried him through life for some forty plus years and he expected it to continue. This time, though, his enemy was an enormous one and had swallowed much bigger and smarter men than Franco. In his headstrong rush to get Juanita, he would take these *federales* and Slocum with him to the fires of hell. Slocum felt ready for a change in scenery. But even untied, he could not figure a way to escape this madness.

Maybe if they found water, maybe then he could consider a way or devise an escape plan. Unconsciously, he reached to his side to adjust his holster. Nothing there. In his deepest thoughts, he accused himself of failing. There had not been a gun on his hip in days. He turned at the commotion going on behind him.

"I can't go on—" The hoarse pleading in the voice grated on him. Looking down, he saw a soldier sprawling on his belly in the dust, reaching for nothing with one arm, dusty hand extended with rosary beads.

"We'll come back for you when we find horses and water." Franco turned to leave as if that was enough, and head bowed, he hobbled off again.

Oaths left the dry tongues of his men. Hard-set eyes glared at his back and then they, too, went on—too weak to carry any comrade, only moments themselves from following his decision to give it up.

Slocum did the same; he went on. He knew, as the remaining men did, that no one would ever come back for Perona. The turkey buzzards would be the only thing to come for him. Even murderers deserved a better way to die.

A while later, they were going down a steep bank into a wide dry wash. The crack of a single pistol shot shattered the silence. Halfway down and not wishing to fall the rest of the way, he halted on a ledge and looked back up at the others above him. No expression of emotion was on their drawn faces. Perona had escaped. Traded one hell for another. Slocum turned back to his task. Then he went on taking guarded steps to make his way down to the diamond-brilliant glittering bed of the dry wash.

Walking in the loose sand deposited by a million monsoon rain showers took more energy than the hard-packed caliche on top. Franco must had led them a half mile down the water course when he stopped and pointed to the lacy shade under some mesquite.

"Take a short siesta."

The men coasted in on their knees, then crawled to the darker ground better sheltered from the unrelenting sun and flopped down. Grateful for any escape from the brutal hiking, they quickly closed their eyes. Slocum joined them. He had neither the strength nor the ambition left to attempt to escape. Using what was left of his strength to get away and have no place to go in this empty severe land would be ridiculous; he could simply die with them. Be lots easier.

18

Nothing to swallow. A knot in his throat, but nothing to swallow it with. Slocum looked around without raising up his head. It was close to sundown. He tried to locate Franco. When he finally sat up and rubbed his burning eye sockets, there was still no sign of the noncom. Had the bastard left them to their own devices? It would not surprise him.

Then he saw something down the wash and walked over to examine the two objects on the sand. They were split open halves of a small barrel cactus. There had been no desert succulents in the miles they'd crossed. Were there more? Slocum looked in a 360-degree turn and saw no more. Franco must have spotted this one, then gave the order to stop, knowing full well the rest of them would fall deep asleep for a long while. That gave the cactus to him.

"What is that?" Hernandez blinked in disbelief at the empty halves of the small barrel cactus.

"A cactus," Slocum said.

"No, no, I know that. Who ate it?"

"Your leader."

"Where is he?" The corporal swung around looking for his boss.

"Gone to get horses and water like he promised Perona."

"You know he left?"

"Hell, no, but I can see he left."

"*Si. Si.* But where did he go?"

"Bigger question. Are there any more damn cacti for the rest of us to eat?"

133

"I never seen one—in days."

"Right, but there was one here. Bound to be more. Send some men back up this wash. Some of us will look down it."

"Sure, sure. Maybe Franco will be back by then."

Slocum took the smaller man by the shoulders and shook him before he could brush off his hands. "Franco ain't coming back. He's gone on his own to find her."

The man frowned at him. "How do you know?"

In disgust, Slocum shook his head looking at the haggard faces of the others. "Franco spotted this cactus and he sent us to sleep so he could eat it for himself and go on."

"That sumbitch," Uvalde swore and the others agreed.

"Slocum says we need to split up and try to find more cactus," Hernandez told the men.

"Where there is one, there usually is more," Slocum said and they agreed. "But we must share them."

Everyone agreed with a nod. He wasn't certain they'd remember the share part when they found one.

"Some are poisonous?" Tomas asked.

Slocum shook his head. "Those taste too bad to even eat."

"I would drink horse piss right now and say it was champagne" Manolito said.

They laughed and took Hernandez's directions to go off on their search. "Be sure to call all of us if you find any," he reminded them.

Slocum and Hernandez went downstream. The corporal read the signs of Franco's tracks and cursed under his breath. Slocum looked up and saw a small cove under the dry wash's tall eroded bank. There, on a raised piece of land, were over a dozen barrel cacti.

"Eeeha!" Hernandez shouted for the others. "And we were only half a kilometer from finding them earlier." He drew out his knife and charged them.

"Be careful, they have sharp needles," Slocum warned.

"Ah, *si*. Very tough fishhook one." He sunk his great knife in the first one. Unlike a watermelon, barrel cacti do not cut easy even under a sharp blade, so Hernandez was forced to use both hands to saw away and finally and split open the cactus. He sliced out some of the green flesh and stuck it in his mouth. Handing Slocum the knife, he smiled.

"Tastes like piss, but it's wet." He chewed and nodded in approval. His tightly drawn face shone orange in the last rays of sundown. "We are saved, no?"

Slocum agreed. "For now."

He chewed on the piece of hot cactus meat. The alkali flavor was bitter but to a man dying for something wet, it was tolerable enough as the liquid spread like irrigation water on dry dirt and soaked into his thick hard tongue. He cut another chunk out as the men rushed in to join them. Handling the knife back to Hernandez, he sat down and chewed on his new source of life.

The men rushed around cursing and chopping at the cactus in a full-blown attack. Hernandez held a piece on the end of his great knife. "The mother of Jesus heard our prayers."

"Remember, she also will give us a bellyache if we eat very much of it."

The corporal stopped before taking the next bite. "How much can we eat?"

"No more than we need to help us get by."

The noncom was on his feet. "Wait! You can get sick and die if you eat too much. Only a little, *mi amigos*."

"What about Franco?" Manolito asked. "He ate two halves."

"I bet he's got a fire-breathing dragon and a kicking mule in his belly right now," Slocum said, imaging the results. It was not the first time he'd eaten cactus for its moisture, but an Apache scout had warned him back then—eat too much and pay the price.

"It would serve him right," Hernandez said, chewing on a smaller piece this time.

They slept a few hours after midnight, then rose rubbing their bellies.

"It don't settle so good," Hernandez said, making faces in the starlight as they began to move out. "Is this wash in the San Pedro drainage?"

"We can hope so," Slocum said.

"If it goes inland we may find the river today."

Slocum agreed and went on down the broad flat bed. It went somewhere and that was where he wanted to be. The cactus only filled a part of his desires. He'd dreamed about being neck deep in cool water. And woke to the smell of creosote and the still-hot breath of the desert. Damn Franco and his greed and obsession for that poor girl. Damn. Juanita must think they'd all forgotten her. That notion sawed on his conscience. He stumbled along in the starlight. His feet were so sore he had no idea how they carried him. Only the need to survive drove him to seek some sanctuary. A place to escape—where was Billie? Where were the wonderful women in his life? Damn. He hoped none of them were in a plight similar to his misfortunes. He was ready to use prayer beads to escape this form of purgatory.

The other men staggered along, stretched out over an eighth of a mile in a train. They believed in the Virgin Mory's ability to intercede for them. Maybe he should take up the faith, too. They'd been delivered to the cactus. Perhaps during this day, still concealed by the darkness of night, they'd find real water; hope for such a discovery sprang in Slocum's heart. But his hardship had somehow destroyed his ability to navigate—that skill was slow to return to him. He could only hope for a speedy recovery. His life depended on it.

Dawn came like slow drawn curtain. They had little to say— march on. Slocum was about to look for another cactus—when a rifle shot slapped the sand. Slocum's heart stopped and he blinked at the figure on the wall of ravine.

"Drop your guns," came the order.

Standing in the sun's rays was Billie Barton, in men's clothing way too big for her. She adjusted a sleeve and smiled with her upper gums showing as she looked over the others. Slocum had known many women—but at the moment Billie was the most beautiful one he could recall ever seeing.

"They won't fight you." He waved his hands at them to put down any resistance, then in admiration looked up at her. "How did you ever find me?"

"Hell, you left your hat back there, a mule, a roan horse and, they say, a dead woman."

He nodded.

"Hawk is bringing you the roan. He tracked you for me."

"If you have some water, toss it down. These men have not had any in a long while."

She nodded. "If that's what you want."

He shrugged, then nodded. "They could have killed me." He heard the drum of horse hooves coming down the wash toward them.

Hernandez coughed and half choked, finally managed to shout to her. "How far to water?"

"I don't know. Ask the Apache bringing Slocum his roan."

The young buck reined up short. Under an unblocked felt hat with an eagle feather trailing off the back, he handed the reins to Slocum. His hard look at the *federales* spoke of his hatred for them and the new Winchester in his right hand looked foreboding.

"How far to water?" Slocum asked him.

"Half a day—" He used the rifle to indicate downstream. "Plenty water."

"Oh, praise God!" one of the soldiers shouted.

It required one great effort for Slocum to put his dead-feeling foot in the stirrup and then mount the roan. Billie was back at the edge of the rim overlooking the troopers.

"Here." She swung out two canteens to toss to them and the *federales* rushed to catch them. Slocum turned on the roan and closed his eyes. Only one thing, he hoped this was not a dream. Then he set the gelding after the Apache.

"Where are your boots?" she asked, looking shocked at his feet. From her saddle horn, she handed him his hat and a large metal water can with a cork lid. "They look infected."

Drinking eagerly from the can, he waved aside her concern. Taking a break and a breath, he slumped in the saddle, knowing the water would churn up his empty stomach later on. "It's a long story. Let's get out of here. You seen Franco?"

She frowned and shook her head. "Where did he go?"

"He found a cactus to eat and left us to die a night ago. I think he's headed for Arispe." Slocum decided the hat hurt his sun-baked head and pushed it off on his shoulders, the tie string at his throat.

"Hawk," she said, swinging in the saddle of a small mustang that fit her, "you see his tracks."

"Big man?"

Slocum nodded.

"He must be at Arispe by now."

Slocum agreed and bobbed his head, then turned to her. "How long have you two been looking for me?"

"I went back to Arizona when they took you. I couldn't get anyone up there to come down here and help me. Mary told me that Hawk had come in and he would be my guide. So I charged these horses at the livery, same for the goods we needed at the store and we came back down here and tracked you down."

Slocum nodded. "You must have meet Don Campos?"

"Yes—ain't he is a strange man? He cries for his daughter and does nothing." She shook her head as they short-loped the horses through the stirrup-high greasewood. "He told us you had killed some soldiers, but you were looking for her and that was all."

Slocum nodded and guided the roan around a deep ravine, then turned in the saddle to ask her to tell him more.

"At the little village, a man who once lived with the Apaches as a boy told us how Franco killed the woman. That was the bad part and how they made you walk. He gave us your horse and we gave him the mule."

"Fine," he said, patting the roan's neck as they drew up to make a decision on how to continue. A deep arroyo blocked their way.

"We have been coming. I knew we would find you when we found their horses dying. Hawk knows this land and can find water in the damnedest places." She smiled at the Apache. "He's a good man."

Slocum nodded he heard her and turned to Hawk. "How do we go from here?"

"You wish to go in the town?"

"No, not till dark."

"I can go in," she said. "No one knows me as a 'boy.' "

Disturbed at the notion of exposing her to either Franco or De Baca, he frowned at the idea. "I don't want you in harm's way."

"You need a doctor to look at your feet. They look terrible and we need to make you some soft shoes."

He wasn't about to argue with her. Some good whiskey might not kill the pain but he wouldn't care if they hurt then. Time for that later.

"I'll ride in," she said. "And find the doctor and then we can slip you to see him after dark."

"Be careful." The notion of her going in by herself disturbed him, but he needed his swollen feet seen about, so he could get around and handle them. A long list—Rojo and Juanita, DeBaca, if need be, and Franco, the butcher. All no doubt intertwined in this matter. And he needed a plan of what to do when he did locate them.

Hawk led them to a secluded spot on the San Pedro River. There was grass for the animals and water—pretty bright water that rushed over smooth rocks inviting Slocum in. He dismounted heavily, and his feet on the ground at last, he let the chills of pain run up his jaw. His feet felt like stubs. Billie was under his arm and supporting him in a flash.

"Can you stand?"

"I can. I'll be fine. Guess we have this place to ourselves?" He looked around under the giant gnarled cottonwoods. The river provided music and dollar-sized leaves spun and clashed from the strong wind in the canopy over them. It was a haven for a million birds, and their songs mixed with the rustling.

"I'm taking a bath and soak." He indicated the stream.

"Hawk, keep an eye out. Slocum's going to take a bath."

The Apache nodded with his arms full of his saddle.

"He'll take care of the horses," she said. "He's a good man. I don't have to tell him much." Helping him walk down to the sandy shore, she acted excited.

"You be damn careful going into town," he said.

She pursed her lips and looked up at him like a forlorned pup. He bent over, took her in his arms and kissed her. A slow deep kiss that simmered like a good fire. The heat began to pulse through both of them. When at last he moved his lips off her mouth, she hugged his neck hard and took a deep breath.

"Oh, Slocum, I worried they had killed you on the trail."

"Aw, no one could do that."

She buried her face in his shirt and shook her head, hugging him tight. "They tried."

"I'd better get in the water."

"Need my help?"

"Naw, I can do it."

"I'll be back in a few hours. You need to sleep. Hawk will guard you."

"I know. You were lucky to get such a good scout."

"He's a good one. You want anything from town?"

"Don't go out of your way, but a bottle of whiskey might help." She winked at him. "I'll see what I can do."

Pulling up her pants by the great belt, sleeves flapping, she ran for her horse. He waited and waved when she was in the saddle, ready to leave and talking to Hawk before she went. Then he began to undress. The notion of sitting on his butt in the water and soaking forever sounded like dying and going to heaven, though he wasn't ready for that trip—yet.

Hawk came down to the water's edge and sat on his haunches, balancing the Winchester over his leg.

"Has Gray Fox gone to San Carlos?" Slocum asked, sitting chest deep in the surging water and scrubbing his heated face with hands full of the cooling liquid.

"He is still trying to get all his people to go north. Geronimo has magic and he has spells on some of the men."

Slocum nodded. He knew the short, hard-eyed medicine man. The One Who Yawns was his name before the Mexicans renamed him Geronimo. No one knew how his leadership had grown so strong. Maybe if Taza, Cochise's son, had been as strong as his father, the lineage of chieftains would have gone on. But the boy never wanted to be a leader, never wanted to resist the whites. He was happy living with two lovely young wives—but Geronimo was never happy. The reservation's rule that you couldn't beat your wife was an invasion of a warrior's personal life. And to be punished for manufacturing the tizwin that was an important part of an Apache's life—how he could get drunk and forget that white men were defecating on the sacred places in Apaches' hearts.

"He is a *brujo*," Slocum said and nodded, wondering if his feet would ever recover from the rough treatment he'd given them. The cool water drew some of the heat from his body.

"We cannot live in Mexico," Hawk said, looking at something distant. "The *federales* have gotten brave and have big numbers. They have invaded the Mother Mountains. Even those once-secret places we used to use are not safe. It would be better to live in San Carlos than here."

"Geronimo expects all the dead Apaches to come back and help him."

Hawk smiled like one did at a small child's fabrication and nodded in agreement. Then he rose and left. His discussion and explanations were over. Slocum knew no one would slip up on him with Hawk watching, so he savored the soaking for a long afternoon.

In time, he climbed out and gamely made his way to a rock slab for the sun to dry his water-wrinkled skin. Then he dressed and limped into the camp. Seated on a blanket, he looked at his swollen feet. They'd require a while to heal. Since nothing was secret in Mexico, the arrival of a "boy," an Apache and a crippled gringo would not go unnoticed for long. Word would be out and available for Rojo, DeBaca and Franco. They needed a base. A place to stable their horses and stay with someone. If he could ride, he could find such a place at one of the small farms that irrigated out of the San Pedro. A widow or older couple needing some income . . . money—his was in his vest. He must have left that behind when Franco took him prisoner. He'd been under such pressure, he'd let lots of important things slide away.

They'd sure need money and he didn't see any money trees among the cottonwoods. Things had begun to pile up. He hoped Billie had made it in and out of town. In the fluttering shadows, he saw his guard on alert, red cloth headband, fresh-cuts bangs and a rifle over his legs a hundred feet away.

Someone was coming. The horses lifted their heads from grazing and nickered softly. Billie'd returned. She bounded off, unhooked a poke from the saddle horn and nodded to Hawk who took her horse. Smiling big, she came across the glen.

"What do you know?"

"I know—" She checked around to see if they were alone. "I have whiskey. A tweezers and a needle to remove the spines, some disinfectant and aloe vera to put on them. The doctor said that was about all he would do."

The poke set on the ground, she dropped to her knees to examine his feet. "Doctor Sanchez said some the spines would eventually work out, but to remove all I could and use the disinfectant and aloe on them every day."

"There must be a thousand." He set back on his hands and shook his hands considering the task. "Hear any word about any of them?"

"DeBaca is at the hotel. His men are out looking, I guess. No word on Rojo and the girl and no one's seen Franco that I talked to."

"You did good."

"You'd better start on the whiskey, this ain't going to be pretty." She began rolling her sleeves up to go to work. Then she leaned forward to hand him the whiskey.

He removed the cork and then smiled at her. "Quit when you get tired." The whiskey heated his ears and he felt it go all the way to his stomach. Oh, this pulling them out business was going to hurt worse than getting them in in the first place. He winced, shook his head and took another swallow. Two more takes at the neck of the bottle and he wouldn't give a damn.

19

His feet coated in aloe, and wrapped in cloth, he awoke to a world of golden red light that gilded the rough barked trees and everything in its touch. It was sundown and he could smell Billie's small cooking fire.

The next morning she redressed his feet, bandaged them, then left and rode to town. He settled in to cleaning the cap and ball .44 pistol from his saddlebags. Hawk squatted near him and watched, getting him anything he needed.

"That old gun shoot good?" Hawk asked, sitting on the ground close by.

"It would kill a snake."

The Apache chuckled. "Call it snake-killer, huh?"

He flexed his arm and nodded. He'd almost forgotten the rattler's bite. Good thing his sore feet sure itched, too. Someone once told him that meant they were healing. It couldn't come fast enough.

In a short while, he finished reloading the pistol, put caps on the five loaded cylinder and rolled it around so the hammer rested on the empty one.

"Where do you live?" Hawk asked.

"Under the stars."

"You have no people?"

Slocum shook his head. "A brother I haven't seen in ten years. My parents are dead. My home place was burned to the ground in the war. Tax collectors took it from my father—"

"No home, no wife, do you not want them?"

"This life's not what I desire. But I'm wanted in Kansas. There is not a place safe for me to stay long."

"If we find the girl, what then?"

"We need to convince Gray Fox to go back with us. Could we do that?"

Hawk nodded. "His heart is not in Mexico any longer. But he would like all of his people to go back, too."

"I am going to take a nap now."

"Sleep, I will keep on the watch." His copper-colored lips pursed tight, he gave Slocum a hard nod.

"Good, then I can rest." He smiled at the young red man. His own strength was returning. Maybe his feet would recover. But his sleep proved troubled. Franco stomped through his dreams again, and because of his feet, he was forced to crawl after him as he raced away on a fast horse. Lost in the dust, Slocum tried to catch up with him, wearing holes in the knees of his pants. Then he woke up in a cold sweat despite the hot wind.

He sat up and looked around. The horses switched their tails at flies, uninterested in anything. His skin trembled under his shirt, but he soon drew a deep breath of relief—it was only a dream.

"You woke up," Billie said and came over with a cup of coffee. "You'll never believe what Hawk and I are doing."

He nodded and took the cup. "What's that?"

"Making you some squaw boots. I don't figure you could get in real boots for a while."

Slocum glanced over at the Apache who was busy with a hunting knife cutting soles out of a piece of rawhide. "Suits me fine. Learn anything more?"

"I overheard two guys talking. They mentioned Rojo and the Norte Ranch."

"Where's that?" Slocum asked.

Hawk looked up and pointed his knife north. "It was deserted last time I was here."

"Good place for him to be."

"Don't get all excited, off of a horse, you'd be like a turtle on his back. Oh, and I did find us a place to stay. Nice widow women. Has corrals and she has hay. It's on the edge of town and she wants four bits a day plus the cost of the hay."

"Can we afford it?"

"I still have money," she said.

"Good," he said and rose to go relieve himself. His feet were still sore, but not as bad as they had been, even though they still must have a thousand needles left in them that she couldn't get out.

"Here," she said and gave him two crutches. "I found them in a store in town."

He nodded in approval and thanked both of them. For supper, they ate some fire-braised beef strips she'd bought in town.

"I told her we'd be there in the morning. Her name is Estrella." Billie looked up from eating as if asking for their okay.

"Sure," Slocum said and looked for the silent Hawk's nod of approval.

"Be fine. Maybe then I can ride up to this Norte place and see what I can," Hawk said.

"Just be on guard," Slocum said, concerned for his safety. "Rojo is a mad killer."

"Me watch for him. Then I be back in a day and tell you what is there."

"Good idea. Take some jerky and hard candy," she said, sounding motherly.

Hawk agreed.

The squaw boots suited Slocum and he was pleased with the fit. He even felt a notch more secure, though crutches were not the best mode of travel in a tight spot. He chewed on the stringy beef and enjoyed it. Much better than half-cooked *pinole* and there was lots more of it.

When the purple light crossed the horizon in the east, Hawk and Billie packed for the move. Slocum stood on his short crutches and bent over to warn the young buck again to watch out; then the Apache leaped on his horse and trotted off to see about the Norte Ranch.

Slocum eased himself in the saddle and nodded to Billie he was ready to leave. She led the two pack horses. His hand went to check the gun butt of the .44. It felt good to be armed again. For a moment, he thought the roan would duck his head and buck— but he talked him out of it.

When the gelding finally settled down, so did Slocum. With a whistle of relief, he set the pony after her and the pack animals. He hoped his plan to board with this woman worked. If only his damn feet would heal up faster.

"You talk to Clayton when you went back?" he asked, riding up alongside of her. "He must think I ran out on him."

"We've been so busy or you've been resting a lot. I forgot to tell you he gave me the money for the trip and said to tell you hi when I found you."

"Bet he's tired of feeding all those Indians."

"No and the townspeople are helping him. Now they can see they mean no harm. Several ranchers have been keeping them in meat, too."

"Guess they figure it's better than them slow-elking one."

"What's that?" She made a face.

"Oh, where you kill a critter and only use a leg or a loin off of it and let the rest rot."

She nodded. "Slow-elking, hmm, I learned a new word. That's a game me and my maw played every day. Learned a new word from the dictionary. She always said, 'Hill folks don't need to be dumb.' "

"Smart woman."

"She'd turn over in her grave if she knew her only daughter ended up like this."

"You ashamed of this?"

"No. I'm more ashamed of how I listened to that lying Fred in the first place."

"We get done, I'll buy you a ticket to wherever you want to go."

She looked over hard at him with her eyes shaded by the straw hat. "You mean that, don't you? I don't doubt you, you're man of your word."

"I'll do my damnedest."

She threw back her head and laughed. "And let me tell you, your damnedest ain't half bad."

"Which way will you go?"

"Can I let you know?"

"Sure, that's fine."

Estrella came running out of the ramada to greet them. She was a short, dark-faced woman wearing an apron over her blouse and full skirt. "You are a big hombre, but I got a hammock will fit you."

"Good," he said and put his crutches on the left side of the roan. At last on his crutches, he nodded to his hostess. Cold chills ran up the side of his facial muscles. He was a long way from being well enough to chase kidnappers and killers.

"*Gracias* for your hospitality," he said to her and tipped his hat.

"I though she was a boy?" she said from behind her hand. "Isn't there an *Indio*, too?"

Slocum chuckled. "Yes, he's gone to get something, may not be back for a day. And Billie is about half boy anyway."

"How you say, tomboy, huh?"

"Yes, but she is sweet."

"Come, you must sit. What pains your feet?"

"I have to unsaddle this horse."

"No." Billie came by and took the reins. "Do as she says."

He shook his head at her and then followed Estrella Sanchez to the ramada, a brush arbor covered in palm fronds. He took a seat on large packing crate.

"Can I see your feet?" she asked.

"They ain't pretty, but the new boots they made are. Oh, yes, what is wrong with them? I walked a long ways in the desert barefooted."

She was on her knees undoing the boot and soon had the left one unbandaged. A concerned look darkened her face. "We must soak them. I have some herbs to bring out the poison. Those needles all have some poison on them and you have much in your system." She undid the other boot. "Do you sleep a lot?"

"Yes, why?"

"The poison does that to you. If you weren't such a grande hombre, you would be in bed, too weak to do anything."

"What does she say about them?" Billie asked after Estrella ran off to get the things she needed.

"Says I'm being poisoned by the needles."

"Hmm, I never heard of that. Guess she knows these desert things. I knew a granny in Arkansas could cure anything with her medicine."

"You may have found another."

They both laughed.

In twenty-four hours, Estrella's hot water soaking treatment showed a marked improvement in his feet.

When Hawk rode in late that afternoon, Slocum put on his boots and hobbled over there to greet him.

"Learn much?"

The Apache looked around as if to check if they'd be heard. "Red-haired one there. Has four vaqueros—pistoleros?" His dark eyes inquired of Slocum looking over the seat of his saddle at him.

"Probably they are."

"Pretty woman is there, too."

"You saw her?"

Hawk nodded.

Juanita Campos. Good, they had to get her out of there. "You did well. Go to the ramada and Estella will feed you. She does that good as she doctors."

"Your feet much better. I see you cross over here." Hawk smiled in approval.

"Much better," he said and dropped his armpits down on his crutches for the trip back. They're healing faster. Not well, but better.

Billie looked up from the skirt she was sewing on for herself. She put it aside when he returned. "Learn much?"

"Yes, she is up there." He sat down on his crate and began removing his boots.

"Well," she said, resetting the skirt over her legs, ready to sew. "You aren't able to run very fast yet."

"But we need to rescue her."

"Tell me how and I'll go do it." She looked hard at him.

"The three of us, a little surprise and catch them off guard, we might do that."

She shook her head in defeat. "When do we go up there?"

"How far away is it?" he asked Hawk who came to squat in the shade.

"Maybe four hours on your clock."

"Estrella," Billie set aside the skirt and called to the woman as she came out of the casa. "Hawk is here. And he's hungry."

"Good. I can feed him."

As the youth ate, Hawk and Slocum talked about the ranch and how it was laid out.

"Rojo and the girl are in the main house. But she takes baths in the tank and swims. No one bothers her or peeks at her either."

"Guess he laid down the law to them. How far is that tank from the house?"

"It is a ways and behind some more buildings." Hawk took another bite of his burrito and nodded in approval at Estrella's food.

"Are the four on guard?"

Hawk shook his head. "No, they played monte all day. I watched them into the night."

"Wonder why DeBaca has not found out about them being up there?" Slocum shook his head. The captain might have a new sergeant less aggressive than Franco. Still, if Slocum, Billie and Hawk knew about the location, DeBaca had to have figured it out by this time, too.

"We'd better be up there by dawn. Time isn't on our side."

"What're you thinking?" Billie asked.

"If we know where she's at, so must the *federales* and Franco, if he's alive."

Billie scowled. "He's alive unless someone hid his head from him."

"You're probably right."

"What do we need for supplies?" Billie asked.

"I guess we're fine. We'll leave the pack horse here and cut our time getting up there. We can get the jump on those vaqueros before they know what happened to them. Then we can take Rojo out or separate her from him somehow."

"Sounds easy to a man on crutches," she said and shook her head in a disgusted way.

"What else can we do?"

"Damned if I know. But you have to remember that you can't run or hardly walk without those sticks."

"I know."

"Hmm, so you realize it—" She went back to her sewing.

They left Estrella's under a sky pricked with stars. The soft clop of their horses awoke several dogs as they passed the dark jacals. Cool air settled around them and the outlines of the hills in the starlight stood out like resting camel humps. Hawk led the way and they trotted up the San Pedro Valley.

Both Billie and the Apache carried new repeating rifles and he had the single shot .25/20 that had been in his gear left at the village. Close to the time dawn threatened, he worried if they should have left Estrella's sooner, but the dark buildings loomed ahead.

"You stay here," Billie said to Slocum, when they reined up to dismount.

"Like hell, I'll be right with you."

"Good," she said and hitched her horse's reins to the mesquite.

They eased up to the jacal. Slocum could hear them snoring, then one coughed, obviously getting up. Hawk held his hand back for them to stop. When the man came out on the dark porch, Hawk busted him in the head from behind with his rifle butt. The bare-assed vaquero went down like a poled steer. Slocum nodded in approval and they slipped inside the dark room.

He held up a finger and pointed at a snoring one for each of them. He set down the rifle and went to the hammock of the first one, jabbed the muzzle of his .44 in his face and said, "One word and you're dead. You savvy?"

"*Si*," came the reply.

In minutes, by the light of small candle, all three vaqueros were bound and gagged on the floor. Then Hawk and her dragged the fourth one inside and did the same to him.

"If you don't make a sound, when we have the girl, I'll come back and turn you lose. You savvy?"

"Mmm," came their answers.

"House is next. So far so good," he said to his partners.

Slocum swung around on his crutches and they headed for the sprawling main house.

"They should stay tied up," she whispered as they hurried across the pearl-lighted open ground.

"Yes," he agreed.

At the back porch he paused to catch his breath. Hawk with his rifle ready went in first. He moved like a shadow and Slocum envied him as he sneaked in behind Billie. The kitchen smelled of mesquite wood smoke and food odors. Hawk paused in the doorway, then waved for them to follow him. Swing by swing, Slocum trailed Billie and they entered the big room. Light spilled in from the open courtyard doors. Hawk stopped to listen at every other door.

Then he indicated with his rifle—the one they must be in. Slocum nodded. He motioned for Billie to move aside and he crossed the gritty tile floor. No sense getting her in harm's way. But he knew she was coming anyway. Hawk tried the latch and the door gave. The creak was small, but it sounded like a train whistle to Slocum.

When he reached the Apache's side, he drew his Colt and gave him a nod. The door swung open and a woman screamed so loud it hurt Slocum's ears. "Indians!"

"Don't reach for that gun," Slocum ordered, but the man on the bed never listened. He dove for his holster hanging on the chair. Slocum's six-gun and Hawk's .44/40, both exploded at the same time. In the room filled with the acrid black powder smoke, everyone began coughing. Billie rushed over to reassure the hysterical Juanita and calm her.

Rojo did not cough. Slocum could see him sprawled on the floor in a heap. Both of their bullets had made fatal holes in his thin chest.

Hawk went and pushed open the French doors to let some air in the hazy room. "I'll go find a horse for her to ride."

"Good idea."

Billie led the still-distraught Juanita into the big room. Slocum hooked Rojo's pistol and holster over his shoulder. He might need it. When he came out of the bedroom, Juanita ran over and hugged him.

"Oh, I didn't know it was you, hombre. Oh, thank God it is you. I have been praying to the Virgin Mary ever since he took me."

He balanced on his crutches and patted her. "You'll be fine now."

"What happened to you?" she asked, moving back and looking at his crutches.

"I can explain later."

"Where did Hawk go?" Billie asked.

"To get her a horse. He'll be back. Let's find some food and get something to eat. Then we can ride out of here."

"I can help," Juanita said.

So the three went into the kitchen. In no time, the fire was going and Billie swung a coffeepot to boil over the flames.

Slocum told Juanita why he was on crutches as the two women worked on the food preparation. He heard horses coming from the corral. Good, Hawk had her a mount. He'd wondered why the Apache had taken so long. If he hadn't been crippled, he'd already have gone to check on him.

Slocum was about to speak to the woman when a hard voice spoke from the doorway. "Don't move!"

No mistaking that raspy, deep-sounding speech. Slocum turned slow-like and Juanita screamed.

"Shut up!" Franco ordered, coming in the kitchen with a double-action service revolver in his fist.

"Where's Hawk?" Billie demanded.

"Ah, there's that little pussy that shot my man and got away." Franco laughed at his discovery of Billie, taking Rojo's holster from Slocum's shoulder, then the .44. "He will have a headache, but I didn't kill him."

"Thanks for taking such good care of them pistoleros for me. They won't bother anyone again." Franco laughed aloud. "And you led me here. So nice of you. I could not have taken this place and got my lovely Juanita without your help, *mi amigo*."

"I am not your lovely Juanita." She stomped her foot.

"Ah, little one, you will be my wife by nightfall."

"No, I won't."

"Yes, and you will like my dick, it is bigger than that boy Rojo's."

"Never. I will kill myself."

"Sit in this chair, little pussy," he said to Billie. "I am going to tie you up. I would kill you, but I don't want my new bride to be upset about that, too."

"You know I'll be coming for you," Slocum said.

"How? I am breaking your crutches, too." Franco laughed even more. "Then you can chase me, huh? Like a dog, no?"

Finished tying up Billie, he laid the first crutch on the table and broke off half of it. Then he did the next one. The whole time, his dark eyes challenged Slocum to move a muscle.

"Come, my *chérie*, we ride for another place and leave them to this filthy casa."

"I won't go—" Her words were cut off when he savagely caught her by the arm and slapped her open-handed. "Another word from you," he said through his clenched teeth, "and you will know better than to sass me."

Juanita held the side of her face and looked in shock at the monster gathering up the weapons in a sack. Finished, he turned and glared back at her. "Get your ass over here with me, girl."

She hesitated, then hurried over to him, looking with pleading, wet eyes at Slocum. Then Franco shoved her hard toward the door. "See you, cripple." He laughed going outside.

"You ever see me again, you'd better have been to confession," Slocum said after him.

"Don't even think about it," Billie said to him, straining at her binds as he started to get up and pursue the outlaw. "Get me loose."

He moved, using the kitchen table to steady himself and drew out his knife to cut her binds. In seconds, she was free. He left the knife on the table and rushed to the door. His rifle was in the bunkhouse. His feet ached and his head swam, but he started out the door in a half run. He could still see Franco riding east. Pain shot into his hips and in ten steps, Billie was under his arm and supporting him.

He could make out the fleeing noncom leading Juanita on another horse. If he could only reach the rifle and kill him. On the bunkhouse porch, he fell down and she helped him up. His hand went around the corner and he felt the hexagon-shaped barrel and pulled it outside.

20

Hawk was alive, which was more than Slocum could say for the vaqueros. The horrific, bloody scene in the bunkhouse was what Billie screamed to him about when he was too late to shoot at Franco.

The army had arrived, a day late and a dollar short. When the bandaged Hawk made a sign there were weapons he could get from inside the bunkhouse, Slocum shook his head.

Leaning forward in the rocker, Slocum nodded to the familiar face of Captain DeBaca. "Get down and rest awhile."

"Corporal Morales, tell the men to look around." DeBaca dismounted and his orderly took the horse. He came with his quirt looped around his right wrist and stopped at the edge of the overhang.

"Look inside," Slocum said with a head toss.

DeBaca stepped up and stood in the doorway. "Who did this?"

"Your man, Franco. He also took Juanita Campos a couple of hours ago and fled."

"I understand your anger. Corporal Hernandez reported to me about his madness and what he did to you and them."

"He has the girl."

DeBaca nodded. "Poor Don Campos is beside himself." The man looked around. "Where is the outlaw, Rojo?"

"Dead in the house. When we burst in, he went for his gun."

"You can leave Franco to us. He will be apprehended and tried for his crimes."

Slocum rubbed his upper legs. His feet hurt anew. "For my

153

154   JAKE LOGAN

money, you can shoot him and let the buzzards have him if you can get her safely away from him."

"All that he deserves. I will leave a detachment to bury the bodies since I see you are still disabled." Debaca nodded to his feet. "Sorry about that."

"I'll be fine some day."

"Corporal Hernandez says you are indestructible to have lived through all that he did to you." DeBaca looked hard at him, then touched his hat brim realizing Billie was a woman standing beside him. "Good day, Slocum and you, ma'am."

Four men fell out as the burial detail and dismounted. None looked pleased at the assignment. A corporal was in charge. No doubt they wanted to be with the column moving out of the ranch yard.

"Where are all the dead?" the Corporal asked Slocum.

"One's in the house. Four in here."

"You kill all of them?"

Slocum shook his head. "Franco did four. We shot one to save the girl."

"They say she is very pretty. A shame he took her."

"The feeling is mutual. We rode a long ways to find her."

The man nodded. "I have heard Hernandez speak of you."

Slocum closed his eyes, he wanted all that ordeal put behind him. "We'll be leaving shortly."

"*Si*, we will bury them."

"Appreciate that."

"I'll get the horses," Billie said. "Or some. I think Franco took your roan."

"Hope he bucks him off." He and Hawk laughed at the notion.

The Apache stood and went along to help her. He gazed across the wide bare yard and watched two troopers carrying the body of Rojo from the casa to his final resting place. One less worthless whelp that should have been drowned as a pup. He'd not be missed.

Franco still filled his thoughts. He would not be easy to forget.

"We found you a big dun," she said, leading two saddled horses around the corner of the building. "He got the roan all right."

"Oh, more reason I don't like him."

She came on the porch to help him get to the horse. "That makes a thousand, don't it?"

"Close to it."

"Where're we going next?"

"Swing by to get the pack horses and go find Gray Fox. We need him and his people at San Carlos."

"You up to all that?" She looked dubiously at him.

"Yes. Can we find him?" he asked the Apache in the saddle when he rode around the corner.

"We can look," Hawk said and grinned.

"Get the pack horses—some supplies and head for the mountains."

She shook her head, then pulled her straw hat up on her head. "And more crutches for you. Damn, you sure are ambitious, Slocum."

"For a man that can't walk?" He smiled and winked at her, then made the effort to mount the dun. In the saddle, he checked the lanky horse. It acted broke anyway. Whether it once belonged to the dead pistoleros or whoever, he had a stout horse under him. Good, he'd need one in the days ahead. They rode out of the ranch headquarters, waving to the soldiers busy digging a common grave for the victims.

It was long past dark when they reached Estrella's place.

21

Late afternoon, close to supper time, Billie returned with the horses in tow and Hawk hurried to help her put them up. They soon returned and she brought Slocum's new crutches to him.

"Never guess what I learned today in town."

"No, what?" Slocum had the new ones under his armpits and tested them by rapping the end on the ground.

"Made from mountain ash. They won't break. Oh, your friend Madison is now running whiskey to the Apaches."

Slocum frowned. "I thought he hated them."

"Well, the hate must have died. They talked about him buying several kegs and paying for them in gold coin before he headed out a few days ago."

"Where did he get the coins I wonder?"

"Probably stole them. They have stage robberies down here all the time, they said."

"I wouldn't put anything past him."

"His good friend," she said to Hawk and wrinkled her nose.

The buck laughed and took his tray of food from Estrella. "Him, a bad hombre."

"My sentiments as well." Then Slocum wondered if the Apache understood his words. "*Malo* hombre."

"Well, he never propositioned either of you. Nasty SOB."

"She likes him, too," Hawk teased and grinned big at her angry face.

"Get lots of sleep tonight," Slocum said, pausing to dislodge a string of meat with his tongue from his back teeth. "We ride out before sunup."

"Yes, slave driver," Billie said between bites and shared a smile with Hawk.

Predawn, there was a purple hue in the east. Billie paid Estrella their bill and they hugged. Then the woman came over and hugged Slocum. "You be careful, big man."

"I will," he promised.

"*Indio*," she said, gathering her skirts to go over to him, she slapped his leg as he sat on his horse ready to go. "I never knew an Apache I liked before." She raised her head up and smiled at him. "But I like you."

He nodded in approval. "You make good food."

"Well, I live here, come see me again." She waved as they rode out.

The shadowy darkness under the towering cottonwoods concealed their passage. A few dogs barked at their passing. They crossed the shallow San Pedro at the ford and began the assent of the mesa to the east. Slocum's plans were to find Gray Fox and coax him back. DeBaca, no doubt, could find Franco and recover Juanita since he was that hot on their trail. Slocum planned to leave justice to Mexican law.

They made camp that night at the base of the Madres. Billie cooked some rice and meat they bought in a small village and tortillas she purchased from a vendor.

"I sure can't make tortillas," she said as they sat and ate in the growing darkness. "And we'll eat lots of beans up here. I don't think there's any butchers where we're headed."

"Might see us a deer."

"Could we shoot it?"

"That small rifle of mine isn't very loud. I think we could make one shot."

"It'll be the only way we'll get any meat."

Slocum nodded and motioned to Hawk. "How far to where Fox might be camped?"

"Maybe one day's ride."

"Good. Sooner we can get him on the move for home the better."

At dawn, they were packed, saddled and ready. Slocum still walked on eggs with his sore feet, but they were better, though he knew in a foot race for ten feet, he'd be dead last. Hawk led the way and they started into the foothills. By midmorning they passed into the junipers and live oak elevation. The Apache found them a nice small stream to take a break at.

Hawk left them to scout ahead. Grateful to have his feet out of the stirrups, Slocum sat on his butt and watched Billie bathe in the stream. Shafts of sunlight coming through the cottonwoods and sycamore canopy shone on her snowy skin and small figure. Birds sang and Slocum about dozed in the serenity.

The horses threw their heads up from grazing and looked to the east. Wide wake, he tried to raise up and search for what they saw or heard.

"Get dressed!" he said to her and picked up the small rifle.

She came running up the hill with her clothing in a wad. "What is it?"

"Get dressed. I don't know."

"I am, I am." She pulled on her pants and then put on the shirt.

Slocum couldn't see anything. Then he heard the horse and could make out Hawk coming through the brush and trees.

"It's Hawk," she said, seated on the ground putting on her shoes.

"Something is either after him or he saw something."

"Yes" She stood up and strapped on the holster.

Making a hard stop, the Apache jumped out of the saddle and ran over to them. "Whiskey trader is camped over the hill."

"Madison?"

Hawk nodded his head.

"How many are there?"

"I see four."

"What do we do now?" she asked.

"Good question. If my feet where healed I'd ride over there, bust up his last keg and send him packing. He ain't worth stuffing."

"You'd do that by yourself?" A grim set to her face, she blinked her eyes at him.

"I could—if my feet—"

"Hawk and me, we'd help you and be your feet." She looked over at the Indian. He nodded and smiled in agreement.

"He look permanently camped?" Slocum asked, considering the offer.

Hawk nodded.

"Then get a stick and show us the camp in the dirt and what we've got to work with over there."

Plans were set. At dawn, they'd be there and take the bootleggers.

The camp sat in a small grove of jack pines. Their picket line of horses and pack animals stretched on the far side where Hawk would come in from. There was one wall tent and an area where the packs and kegs were piled in the center. Several of the burros had begun braying at the first light. A woman was up stirring the fire and clanking pots.

Slocum pointed out the various men's locations to Billie, whispered that he felt Madison was inside the tent. With a hard look at him, she nodded.

He leaned on his crutches for some last minutes of reprieve. He intended to leave the supports against the nearby pine and go the rest of the way on his own.

"You cover that last one out there on the right," he said. "The rest Hawk and can cover."

"Got him."

He acknowledged her words, put the crutches aside, then drew his Colt. Time to get it on. Careful as he could, he made his way down the slope. The woman at the fire might look up any minute and see him. It would be too late if she did. Hawk had the first guy up on his side—without a sound.

He reached the third bedroll and gave the form under the thick cotton blanket a sharp stomp. "Don't make a sound, hombre."

"Huh?"

"Hands up, get up or die."

"I don't wish to die, senor."

"Good, 'cause we have the rest of you covered. Where's Madison?"

"Ah, in his tent I guess."

"All right, get walking," he ordered the one-piece underwear-clad man toward the fire.

"But my boots?" The man held out his hands toward them.

"No boots. Get walking." Slocum could see Billie was marching her captive in, too. Good so far.

With the three men and woman seated on the ground close to

the fire, Slocum headed for the tent. At the open flap, he could make out someone sleeping on a cot. Satisfied there was no one else in there, he stepped inside and hobbled over to his man.

"Make a dumb move and you're dead."

Bleary-eyed, no doubt from drinking too much the night before, Madison raised up and blinked at him in disbelief. "What the fuck—"

"We've come to have a little party. Get up slow-like and don't try nothing."

"Why—what do you want? I know you. You ain't the damn law down here. What're you after me for?" The ex-scout held his hands out as if to keep Slocum away.

"Selling whiskey to Geronimo only makes him meaner."

"Is that my fault? I'll cut you in on a half partnership . . . three-fourths?"

"I ain't into no partnership with you."

"Listen, Slocum, we can make some big bucks, I mean big ones. Geronimo's got lots of gold money."

"Shame he ain't going to have any whiskey to buy."

"Oh! No!" Madison pulled at his own hair with both hands and clenched his teeth. "Don't do this to me!"

"You try me, Madison, and you'll be feeding the buzzards." He shoved his gun hand forward at the man.

"I'll get even," Madison mumbled.

"Fine, right now all of you start walking," Slocum said and gave a head toss to the west.

"But our boots, senor?" one of the men begged.

"Walking barefoot gives you something to think about. Like not selling damn Apaches whiskey."

"I would never do it again if you'd only let me have my boots and clothes."

"Get hiking."

"I'll kill you for this!" Madison shouted back at him as they stumbled along in a pack.

"Keep walking or I'll go to shooting at you."

"No, no, senor, we are walking," the one in the back said to appease him.

"What now?" Billie asked.

"Pile it up and burn it."

"Saddles and all?" she asked.

"All their gear."

"I want a better saddle," Hawk said, looking them over.

"Fine, pick one out and we burn the rest."

"You'd better sit down," she ordered. "We can do this."

"All right," he said, grateful at the prospect to get off his feet. He kept a sharp eye on the hillside that Madison and his underwear-clad army went over. Without arms, he doubted they'd try to come back.

In an hour, the stack of pack saddles, riding ones, panniers, boots, bedrolls and several small kegs of whiskey were heaped in a pile. The guns, ammo and valuables were packed on one of the saddle horses taken from the picket line. Two kegs were chopped open with an ax and Hawk poured the aromatic liquor over the stack. He dropped the last keg when it was empty and scrambled off.

"Here's to Geronimo," Slocum said and snapped a match alive with his thumbnail. When he tossed it on a whiskey-soaked blanket, it flared on fire and soon the entire mound was ablaze.

Billie with her hands on her hips, nodded in approval

"Cut the burros and horses loose. We need to move on," Slocum said.

"It's hard work doing good deeds," she said with a laugh and hurried over to help Hawk run off the stock.

In a short time, they were on the move again. A column of dark smoke cut the azure sky when Slocum looked back.

"You'd better watch that Madison," she said. "He'd shoot you in the back over this."

"He'd better make it good the first time."

She laughed. "Ain't much ever worries you, does it?"

"Things that worry me are if DeBaca has caught Franco by now and saved Juanita. And if Gray Fox will go to San Carlos with the ones he has."

"Surely DeBaca has her by now."

Slocum shook his head. "Don't underestimate Franco. He's mean, but he also has a calculating mind. He must have been observing us to have followed us to that ranch."

"I think he was there watching them," Hawk said. "When we came back."

"Might have been, but he let us do the dirty work, then he stepped in."

"You said that he was smart."

"If he can outwit DeBaca, he'll sure try."

"Shame those Apaches cooking his brain like you said, didn't finish the job."

"I think all they did was make him meaner." Slocum booted the dun horse up the steep trail. It was narrow enough they were forced to ride single-file as they wound up into the Madres.

Horses sweaty and hot from the long pull, they rested them on a bench where the cool afternoon breeze swept Slocum's face. Big change from the desert where any form of wind was a fiery breath. He studied the pines and mountain mahogany, a red-barked bush that grew in the mountains. Behind them and far below was the desert, with its heat waves and dust. He savored the mountain air.

"We can make a camp on a small stream," Hawk said. "And I will go look for Gray Fox."

"Good," Slocum said as he watched Billie return from the brush. "You ready to go on?"

She narrowed her eyes in the shade of her straw hat and grinned, exposing her missing teeth. "That's what I came for." Pulling up her sleeves, she remounted and they followed the Apache.

"You never told me how you lost your teeth."

"I was maybe ten. We had a bad wagon wreck in Arkansas. I must have been thrown hard, cause I came to spitting blood and teeth. Been gone so long now I only notice when I look at myself in a mirror. Kinda makes me ugly, don't it?"

"No." He shook his head. "When you stood on that bank and rescued me in the desert I thought you were the prettiest sight in my entire life."

"Aw." She blushed. "You was too easy to please that day."

"No, you are one neat bundle of a woman."

"I don't know about that. But it sure is pretty up here. How many white women ever been up here you think?"

"Not many."

"Good, I can say some day, when I was young I rode into them Sierra Madres and they were pretty as heaven. And there weren't many women ever saw them before me."

Slocum agreed with a nod and sent his horse in a trot to catch up with Hawk.

Before the sun formed a ball of fire in the western sky, Hawk led them into a side canyon that was filled with the sounds of rushing water. Under the brow of a high brown rock bluff, they rode uphill on a narrow trail and finally emerged into a bowl. The silver thread of a waterfall spilled off a lip into a green-blue pool and then rushed off down the mountain in the noisy stream Slocum'd heard riding up there.

"Damn!" she swore and whistled impressed. "This is sure nice."

Slocum gave his approval to Hawk. "Good place to camp."

"There is a way out," Hawk said and pointed to a game trail that went up the side of the mountain and into the pines.

Slocum thanked him, studying the thin line and knowing it would be a tough pull if he ever needed to use it. "This is a good place. Do the Apaches use it?"

Hawk shook his head. "No, it is why I brought you here. It is a place of the owl."

"Are you afraid to be here?"

Hawk shook his head. "I trust your medicine. That one never hurt me at the woman's casa."

"Good," Slocum said. "I will keep my medicine strong for you."

As if satisfied, the Apache nodded and began unloading the pack animals. "Go sit. Your feet still hurt you," he said and waved Slocum away.

He needed no more encouragement than that. He went to the site where she wanted to build her cooking fire and plopped his butt on the ground. His squaw boots out before him, hands on his hips, he stretched the tight muscles in his back. His feet were getting better, but by nightfall they always ached. Especially after all the times he'd mashed them down in the stirrups to avoid falling off his horse into some deep gorge.

In a short while, she came dragging in a dead tree limb and handed him the ax. "I'll go get some more."

"Good, I'll have this one chopped up by then."

She leaned over and kissed him on the cheek. "I sure like this place. Maybe we could stay here forever."

"I doubt you'd like eating pine bark and roasted rocks."

"If you were here, I'd like it."

He shook his head and went to chopping the branches up.

Soon Hawk brought in a big armload. His stack of usable fuel grew until she returned with another large fallen branch. Then she began to build herself a pile to make a fire. Hawk brought in some pieces big enough to burn all night.

A lighted match stuck in her kindling set things to burning. As the heat reflected off the fire into his face, Slocum nodded in approval. She drove in her iron stands and soon swung a coffeepot over the fire. He closed his eyes, laid on his back and napped.

She woke him and squatted down, holding a cup of steaming coffee. "Want to sleep or have this?"

He raised himself up on his elbows and grinned at her. "Coffee sounds wonderful. Smells that way, too."

"We'll eat in a short while."

"I'm fine." He sat up and took the cup.

"Hawk's gone to look for his people."

Slocum nodded. "Good."

"He took some jerky and left."

Slocum blew on the coffee. She remained there on her haunches not moving. Something was bothering her and he met her gaze.

"Your feet feeling any better?"

"Some. Why?"

"Cause you ain't—well, been very friendly."

He laughed and set the coffee aside. "I sure never meant to not be friendly," he said and held out his arms to her. She chewed on her lip, then she dove on him. Her mouth on fire attacked his. With her a-straddle of his lap, he reached over and felt her small hard breast through her shirt. Wanting more, she shoved her chest at him. He closed his eyes to savor her fury. Then he unbuttoned her shirt and in seconds, she was on her knees, feeding him the rock-hard nipple and moaning for more.

The taste of sugar filled his mouth and intoxicated his brain. Imagined or not, she tasted like honey. And she soon switched him to the other side.

At last, she stood up. "I'll get us a bedroll." Her shoes hit the ground running and she returned in seconds and unfurled it. In the fire's light, he watched her remove her britches and the orange light dance on her shapely legs. He'd undone his squaw boots and set them aside, then slid off his pants as he sat on the blankets His shirt unbuttoned, she came and pushed it over his shoulders. Her face lowered close to his, they kissed and she settled in his lap.

In seconds, she pushed him down on the blankets and scooted back, raising up to insert him. Then with a cry, she slid down his pole. Bouncing up and down, she soon had both of them straining. He lifted his butt up to meet her attack, savoring the swollen walls and ring. Their actions grew wilder and wilder. Until he felt the stirring in his testicles and he pulled her down hard with both hands clutching her small hard butt. The explosion came and she threw her head back and shouted.

He fell into a dull land of exhaustion. She spilled on top of his chest, hugging him and the pointed nipples drilled holes in his skin. Arms locked around her, he hugged her tight.

"Oh, my God, the food," she said and jumped up.

Slocum raised up and chuckled. Who needed food anyway? Then he heard the owl hoot. Not once, but several times.

She gave him a sharp look as she stirred her kettle in the nude. "That mean anything?"

"Yes, an owl is hooting. Or he sees you and is asking who-who is she?"

"Guess only you would recognize me naked. Fred always wanted to do it under the covers. I guess he didn't like to look at my body."

"I do."

She smiled. "I know and I'm glad. Make's me feel, well, like a woman—oh, there he goes again."

Slocum nodded and listened hard over the sounds of the rushing water. He hoped it wasn't bad news the bird was broadcasting.

22

Hawk did not return by the next morning. The notion niggled Slocum, but he let her drag him to the pond to swim and bathe. They made wild passionate love on the grass and then bathed again. She washed and hung their clothes to dry on the willows.

"If he doesn't come back what should we do?" she finally asked, using a blanket for a shawl.

"Time is not important to an Apache. He'll be back when he gets through. No telling, he may have a woman with him."

Insects began to chirp again. The stream sounded much louder and he could see in the twilight how the waterfall had doubled in size. A count of the horses told him they were all still there.

He turned an ear and listened. A metal ring? Something—he'd heard it. Someone on a shod horse was coming up the trail. He hurried to the tent, his feet hurting at very step. "Someone's coming."

"Who?"

"I hope it's Hawk."

His hand on the gun butt, he wondered if he should hide Billie.

"I can't see anything," she said, coming out of the tent.

He saw them emerge. Two people riding double? He drew his Colt and squinted hard to recognize their outline.

"Ho, Slocum, don't shoot. It is Hawk and my woman."

"Woman?" Billie gulped.

Slocum shrugged. "Come in. I didn't know who it was. We'll build up the fire. You must be soaked."

"Plenty wet." Hawk laughed and jumped down, then reached up to catch her.

"Meet my bride, White Flower. But they call her Blanco."

The young girl didn't look up but nodded slightly as he introduced them. "She has never known any white people. But she will, huh?"

"Yes," Billie said, taking her hand. "Come Blanco. I think I have an extra shirt you can wear for dress while yours dry."

Hawk nodded in approval and shooed her off with Billie.

"Pretty girl," Slocum said, seeing the boy was about to bust with pride.

"Yes. Oh, Gray Fox sent word. He and some of the others will meet us in three days on the Black Fork."

"Is that far away?"

"No, a few hours ride."

"I can't make any treaties." He felt better warning him; all he was was an interested citizen.

"He knows that and knows that you have cared for his women and children."

"Good, maybe we can get this over and get headed back."

"I am ready. Where did she go?"

"She's at the other tent with Billie changing."

"Oh, you make good tent. It really rained."

"Yes, it really rained." Slocum wondered about the boy's adventures over the past forty-eight hours. Came back with good news and a bride—oh, well, maybe he could get on with his own life when this was over.

What was that? His own life, meant running from two Kansas deputies. He'd sleep this night with a pretty gal, his belly was full and he really had no problems—not since Gray Fox had agreed to meet him. Damn. Sometimes a guy didn't know when he was well off.

23

Slocum sent the big dun horse down the slope. The trail narrowed. It dropped off sharply with lots of free air and a pair of harpy eagles floating over it and screaming at his party's free admission to this canyon. Hawk was a few hours ahead of them. Single-file, Slocum and the two women brought the four pack horses with them. This was the Black Fork Canyon. His horse picked his way gingerly and Slocum didn't try to rein him or hurry him. An obvious mountain horse that knew how to handle such situations; Slocum trusted its judgment and skills.

Half an hour later, they reined up and rested the horses on a bench. Both girls ran off behind some bushes and he pissed on the far side of the animals. Nothing was in sight. The open jack pines were thicker in places and even from the edge of the bench, he couldn't see the stream contained far below at the base for the rock outcroppings and the timber.

They mounted up and began their journey once more. Soon the silver stream began to show and he could hear it at times crashing over rocks. A blue jay scolded them, along with the black and white magpies and big ravens.

Midmorning, they met Hawk and he showed them to the grounds along the stream.

"No one is here yet?" Slocum asked, looking over the timbered slopes for any signs of Gray Fox.

"They will come."

"Good," he said. "Should we unpack?"

Hawk nodded.

"If you think there will be trouble, I won't unpack." Slocum did not feel that confident in Hawk's answer.

"Geronimo may come."

Slocum nodded. "You don't know how he'll act, huh?"

"He is a hard man to know."

"Well, we're into this now. May as well unpack. He wants to kill us then we can't stop that."

"Unpack?" Billie asked and at his nod jumped off her horse. Blanco came around and took their horses' reins to lead them off.

"Now we wait," Slocum said.

"They will come."

With a look at the mountains again, he agreed and sat on the ground. This might be a long day.

Hawk must have known for a rider on tall sorrel horse came up the meadow. He wore a skullcap like most medicine men, two holsters and a rifle over his lap. But his dark eyes could have bored a hole in a steel plate.

He rode up within fifty feet, stopped and began to speak in clear Spanish. "You must be the white man."

Slocum nodded, with no inclination to stand up for him. "My name is Slocum."

"Once you were in Nantan Lupan's camp. I remember I saw you there."

"I did some scouting for Crook." Slocum looked off to the river wishing he had some hooks and line.

Geronimo dismounted and gave the reins to Hawk. They spoke a few words in Apache and then Geronimo laughed, no doubt at the young man's expense. On the ground, he was a short man. He strode over and sat down.

"I cannot speak for the army or the White Father," Slocum said.

"I wish to meet him, the White Father. You know him?"

"No." Slocum shook his head. "I am no chief of the white people."

Geronimo smiled as if he knew this was a lie. "You got them food, those women and children."

"Good people don't let good people starve."

Geronimo shook his head. "Many feed my people poison."

"Some Apaches kill women and children for no reason."

"How can we end this?"

Slocum closed his eyes. "If I had the power, I would tell you. I only came to ask Gray Fox to join his people and go to San Carlos as we agreed."

"Will they punish him?"

"I don't know—I will tell them he came on his own. That should be good enough."

Geronimo nodded that he'd heard him.

"Why didn't Gray Fox come?"

"Some of his men are with me. They wanted me to meet you and find out if you lie."

"I don't lie. I don't tell people things I cannot deliver."

Geronimo did not answer or ask any more questions. They sat there and let the cottonwoods rustle, birds sing and the steam rush by.

"Are your feet healed?" he finally asked.

"You know about my feet?"

The small man nodded. "There was a rope around your neck and you walked for many days in the desert without shoes."

"Who told you?"

"I saw it in a vision."

"Is the man who did that to me still alive?"

Geronimo shrugged with no answer. "I will look for him."

"Fine. What will you tell Gray Fox's men?"

"You are strong man, but you are not from the White Father."

Slocum nodded—that was all he could do.

Geronimo put out his hand and shook Slocum's. "We will meet again."

"Yes, thanks for coming. That man—I need to know if he still lives."

"Apaches couldn't kill him." Geronimo laughed. "Maybe a big man like you can."

"What did he say?" Billie asked as Geronimo went to Hawk and took his big horse. Someone rich must miss that sorrel gelding, and Slocum decided he would have loved to own him.

Geronimo left the meadow in a flat-out race for the timber.

Slocum turned back to her and shook his head. "He is a *brujo*, all right."

"What did he say?"

"I guess he came to check me out. All I could tell him was I wasn't sent by the great White Father."

She made a pained face. "Did that hurt or help us?"

"We'll have to see. Obviously, some of Fox's men are with him and they wanted to know who I was." Slocum shook his head, still in a quandary about the visit. "I guess time will tell us if we've won or lost."

"Hawk, you know his purpose?" she asked the Apache when he joined them.

"Geronimo is a strange man. He has much medicine, but if he didn't respect Slocum's, he would have sent his braves to kill him."

"That's how he knew about my feet."

"He did?" She blinked her eyes at him in disbelief.

"He can see things that happen miles away," Hawk said.

"I wonder what he'll learn about Franco?" Slocum shrugged and headed for their camp. "I asked if he was still alive."

She swung on his arm. "You weren't afraid were you?"

"Didn't have time to be."

"Isn't Fox coming here, too?"

"Better ask Hawk, he's the man."

"Gray Fox said he would come here. I never talked to Geronimo."

"Look at that sky. We'd better make a couple of tents. Be some more showers by afternoon." Slocum was observing the fluffy clouds beginning to gather and grow.

They made three tents and were finishing when the first threat of thunder rumbled in the south. The women served reheated beans and Blanco's flour tortillas. They were seated on logs busy eating them, when Slocum saw the first rider come out of the timber.

"We got company."

Hawk nodded and never looked up from his eating. "Gray Fox is coming to see you and his men. They will do you no harm."

"Do we have food for them?"

Billie frowned. "We can make some if the rain don't put out the fire."

Hawk shook his head. "They can wait till the rain is over to eat."

"Good," Billie said, looking uncomfortable.

Slocum rose and finished his burrito. Then he started over to meet the chief. Fox wore a Mexican shirt and a poncho. The eagle feather in his hair twisted in the wind humming through the pines.

"Been many days," Fox said and he threw his leg over so he could slide out of the saddle.

"Many days. How have you been?"

"I worry for my children and the women."

"They were fine a week ago, when she was up there." He indicated Billie who stood by the fire.

"Hawk said so, too." Fox crossed his arms over his chest.

"I told the man who is responsible for them I'd find you and bring you back so all of you could go to San Carlos together."

"Some of my people wish to stay here. I have talked long hours. I am tired."

"Geronimo was here and talked to me a few hours ago."

"What did he say?"

"Asked me if the Great White Father sent me. I told him, no."

"He asked me what kind of man you were. I told him you were straightforward with me and had protected my women and children."

"Fox, I am a man of few words. My feet are in bad shape and I'd like to go back to Arizona. I can't say what the army will do, but if you don't come in, they will probably take them to San Carlos without you."

Gray Fox nodded. "We can't go in all at once. The *federales* and the guardsmen would catch us. We will meet you in four days on the San Pedro on the American side."

The first hard raindrops began to pelt him on the hat and shoulders. Slocum nodded. "In four days on the San Pedro. You can come to my tent."

"No, I have much to do." His words were drowned out by the thunder.

"In four days!" Slocum shouted and ran for the tent in the cold deluge.

At last on his butt and inside, he drew a deep breath.

"What did he say?" Billie shouted over the small hail beating the canvas sides like a drum.

"Four days! On the San Pedro across the border! He'll meet us there!"

She jumped up on her knees and gripped his face so she could smother him in kisses. "Thank God!" she said over the storm's fury. "We're going home at last!"

They fell over on the blanket and became lost in passion's own storm, ignoring the slashing rain outside. His hips plunging into her. Her efforts as wild toward him. They went into a whirlpool and were swept away.

24

Hawk knew a way. Three days, maybe less and he promised they'd be there. By midday, they were out of the fog and the mountains' cool winds. Hawk's trail proved easy compared to many routes Slocum could recall. They'd be on the desert floor by nightfall and then they could scoot northwesterly.

The Apache found them water for their horses. It was stagnant-tasting after the mountain streams, but the thirsty, sweaty horses never complained and drank their fill. The women built a fire and cooked the evening meal while the men saw about the animals. The sun was a fiery glow sinking under the horizon when they finished.

"If we can make Valle by late afternoon tomorrow, maybe we can buy some meat and not hear them complain," Slocum said with a head toss toward the women at the fire.

Hawk agreed.

Behind the water tank, Billie was on her back reloading her Colt. An angry scowl was written on her face. "You see any more?"

Slocum shook his head. "Keep down, it ain't over yet."

"Those no-good bastards shot my horse."

"Bet they wish they hadn't done that."

"They're going to wish a lot more," she said, rolling over, then raising up and joining him. "Who is it?"

"Come out with your hands up," Slocum ordered. "Or get ready to die."

"Senor, I am shot bad—"

174

"He in the cantina?" Slocum asked Hawk.

The Apache nodded.

"Who are you?" Slocum shouted.

"Miquel—Miguel Quares."

"Who do you work for?"

"Senor—Senor Madison."

"Where is that slimy son of a bitch?"

"He rode away—"

"That's like him. I'm coming across to you. Tell the others they want to live to throw out their guns."

"Slocum, be careful," Billie said.

A six-gun from the man between the building flew out, followed by a mustached man with his hands in the air. Another came out of the store with his hands hands held high.

"Watch that other cantina," Slocum said, under his breath to Hawk. The hot sun bearing down, he crossed the baked caliche ground. The .44 in his fist was cocked and ready with three shots left. Thirty steps from the well, Hawk's Winchester barked and another Mexican staggered out of the batwing doors with his six-gun in his hand; he crumbled facedown on the stone walk.

"Where did he go? Madison?"

Quares shook his pale face. "Norte . . . he said it would be . . . easy. He lied. . . ."

Slocum nodded. Madison did that a lot. He closed the man's eyelids.

Out of breath, Billie busted in the doors. "We only got two. Are there any more? Oh, is he dead?"

Slocum stood up and nodded. "Where are all the towns people?"

She stopped. "You hear that yelling?"

"I do," he said.

"I think they're coming back."

Men and woman alike came shouting and waving. Children big and little tried to keep up and their yellow and black dogs barked in excitement as the mob swept in the square.

"You killed them! You killed all of them!" an excited woman shouted at Slocum looking at the dead man who had fallen through the porch roof.

"Let's say we sent some to hell."

"Senor, we appreciate your bravery." A small man wearing an apron came running up.

"You got any meat?" Slocum asked him.

"No, but I can butcher some goats."

"Good," he said, holstering his .44. "Let's have a fiesta!"

"Yes, yes," came the chorus.

People began to dance in the street. Slocum put his arm on Billie's shoulder. "You got that new outfit to wear?"

"Sure, why?"

"Dig it out. We're having a fandango here tonight."

"What about these two?" Hawk asked.

"You got a jail?" Slocum asked.

The head shakes told him enough.

"Take off your boots and all your clothes," he said.

"Here?" the mustached one blinked in disbelief.

"We only got two choices, since they don't have a jail—turn you loose or shoot you at the wall. Which one you like the best?"

"Turn us loose."

"Then undress and you ever come back here again, they'll shoot you."

"But what will we do—"

"Run like hell for a new country. Now get undressed or I'll pick a firing squad."

"No, no, we'll leave."

Naked, they acted embarrassed by their exposure and held their hands over their privates after some catty remarks—dogs were better hung than they were. Taken to the east side of town, Slocum fired his pistol off and the two streaked down the wagon tracks full steam. And every hundred feet or so of the race, Slocum shot again to convince them to hurry and they did.

Drinking wine and eating barbecued goat with Billie seated by him at a long table set up in the square, Slocum greeted the well-wishers. People came by and thanked him for running the outlaws off. Many had to laugh at his justice.

Down the table, Hawk and his bride nodded at their words of praise. Blanco was emerging some, Slocum noticed. When a young girl gave her a white lace shawl as a gift, she rose and hugged her.

The music played on the trumpet, the fiddle and guitar sent dancers whirling away. Many of the songs Slocum had heard before in this borderland, but he was unsure of the title of the songs.

Late in the night they were led to hammocks in a backyard and they thanked their host.

"We aren't sleeping in two of them, are we?" she asked, shedding her skirt.

"No," Slocum said and laughed taking off his squaw boots. "You know, you were one of the prettiest girls there tonight."

She laughed. "You're too easy to please. We'll sleep in your bed."

"Fine."

25

A day early, they made camp on the San Pedro under the towering cottonwoods. Hawk made some wide scouts, but saw no sign of their expected guests. Slocum bought three big steers to butcher from a trader coming through. That depleted the last of Billie's funds and so they waited.

Hawk shot a mule deer on the western slopes of the Huachucas and brought the fat doe to camp. The butchering kept them busy into the night. Later they licked greasy fingers as they ate the cooked meat, which brought four smiles to the forefront.

The next morning, Slocum kicked around their camp.

"Concerned?" Billie asked, bringing his fresh coffee.

"Oh, you never know about Apaches and what they think. An owl can hoot and they'd turn around and go back to the Madres. I'm just unsure. I'd like to get this over."

"And leave me?"

"No, I'd dread that the worst. But we've got a deal. I'll put you on a stage east or west. Which way—" He stopped to listen to the drum of hard-driving hooves.

Slocum gave her the coffee, jerked up a Winchester, levering a cartridge in the chamber. He was trying to see the rider coming through the chaparral.

"That's Hawk riding in on fire," she said about the blur of dust coming off the far ridge.

"Army's coming!" Hawk reined up his sweaty horse and threw his arm back at the Huachuca.

Slocum could see the column of dust and nodded. Damn, all

he needed was the damn army there. What would he do? Did they know about his deal, too?

Guidons flashing, they came at soft lope and the formation stopped short of Slocum, making a great wave of tan dust go off toward the Whetstones.

"Ah, that you Slocum?" the officer asked, pushing his horse in closer.

"Captain Oliver Blake. I didn't know you were going to command buffalo soldiers."

"I wasn't until that damn stage broke down. I lost two days and was late at Fort Grant so they gave my command there to another and when I arrived all they had left was this outfit in the Ninth." He removed his hat for Billie who wore her boy's attire. "Still keeping bad company I see."

"Thank you, Captain. Liking the desert I suppose?"

"Not really." He turned to Slocum. "We understand a band of renegades is coming up here to cross the border and raid the countryside."

"That's wrong. Gray Fox and some of his men are coming back, I hope, to join their women and children and go to San Carlos."

"How would you know that?"

"I made the deal."

Blake folded his arms over his chest. "There are eighty thousand U.S. troops in Mexico, Arizona and New Mexico Territory looking for them and you found them?"

"Their women and children have been camped up at Crystal Springs for two weeks."

"I heard they can't decide who's jurisdiction they're under up there, so no one has gone to get them. Fort Grant says Bowie should go. Bowie claims all their troops are in the field and they can't spare enough men to do it."

Slocum sighed. "Good thing, those folks up there are feeding them. Now if you will repair a few miles downstream, maybe the Apaches will come in. Then you can escort them—if you have the authority—along with their families to San Carlos."

Blake laughed out loud. "Why, Slocum, for the Ninth Cavalry to do anything like that would piss folks off clear to San Francisco. Might even jab Sherman in Washington."

"You saying you won't?"

"Hell, no, you tell me how and I'll listen. I want the job."

"Captain Blake, you have a deal."

The sun set on day four. No Apaches. Hawk could not find any sign of them below the borders. Slocum was beside himself. Where were they?

"I'd better ride up and tell Blake to stay put for another twenty-four hours."

"I'll go along," Billie said and rushed off after their horses.

Hawk agreed. "I think they are coming. Gray Fox hates Mexico. He told me if we stayed down there they would kill the Apaches one by one until we all were dead."

"Cross your fingers and your heart," Slocum said to him and tossed his saddle on a bald-faced horse with a good running walk that he had acquired from the last bandits. No need in leaving a good one behind; they didn't need the horse.

The found the buffalo soldiers' camp and they were challenged by a guard.

"Here to see Captain Blake," Slocum announced and the soldier let them by.

"Well, if it ain't the ambassador to Sonora," Blake said, from the doorway of his lighted tent. "Good evening, Slocum."

"I'm still waiting. Give me twenty-four hours. They may have had trouble. Mexican army is running all over down here too."

"Fine, we love sitting on our asses and eating hard tack and beans. At the fort we'd have to polish leather, shoe horses and do a lot of work; this camping out suits us fine. Don't it, Sergeant Washington?"

"Done suits me fine, sir." The tall black noncom snapped to attention when he spoke.

"Get down off your horse. My men will take them. Have a drink."

"I will and thanks for your patience." Slocum stepped down lightly, his feet were not through hurting. "Curly Madison isn't over at your fort, is he?"

"I haven't seen him since the stage broke down."

"He was in Mexico a week ago trying to sell whiskey to Geronimo."

"Oh, nice guy. No, I haven't missed him either. How are you, Miss—"

"Billie. And I haven't missed him."

"Billie and a young Apache with us saved my life in Mexico."

"I see. Come in my office. Sorry it is not paneled in oak."

Slocum laughed and Billie smiled. They ducked and went in to sit on the canvas chairs. Some night millers flittered and danced in the candlelight and the men drank whiskey.

"Do you really think that he is coming?" Blake said, back in his seat.

"I think he had every intention."

"Good, we'll wait. And you, missus, is it?"

"I'm Billie."

Blake smiled. "I understand that—Billie. I guess you're tired of this desert by now?"

She shook her head. "No, Captain, I'm not. It's been an adventure I shall never forget."

"Well, that's different. Most women hate this country."

"I ain't most women." She suppressed a smile.

"No, ma'am, you are not."

They finished their drinks and Slocum shook his hand. "For better luck tomorrow."

"Yes, much better."

The two rode back to camp. Slocum was absorbed in his own concerns about the arrival or non-arrival of the Apaches. Clayton at the mine must be getting put out over feeding half the tribe all this time.

"They'll come," she said, riding beside him in the starlight. Her hand patted his arm and he managed to smile at her.

"Guess I need your faith."

"I know it will work."

They unsaddled in camp and Hawk came cradling his rifle.

"See anything?" Slocum asked.

"Nothing."

"I guess they're coming." Slocum set the saddle down on the horn and raised up, listening to the night symphony of the insects sizzling around them.

Hawk nodded.

"Wake me up and I'll stand lookout half the night."

Hawk agreed and moved away.

"What's happening?" Slocum whispered.

"Someone is here to talk to you."

"Who?"

"His name in Apache is Stone Face."

With his squaw boots on, Slocum nodded to Billie who was on her elbows in the bedroll taking it all in. "I'll be back."

He strapped on his holster and buckled it. "What does he want?"

"Buffalo soldiers worry them."

"No, they are here to protect them and get them safely to San Carlos."

"You can tell him."

"Is Gray Fox around?"

"He never said, but I think so."

"Good."

The short Apache squatted in his knee-high boots with a rifle balanced across his legs.

"How are you?" Slocum asked him in Spanish.

"Good. Why are the soldiers here?" He gave a head toss in the pearly light toward the north.

"To protect you."

"Gray Fox says you are a good man who speaks the truth."

"Tell him they are here to get you and your people safely back to San Carlos."

"Gray Fox does not trust them, but if you will go along he will join you."

"He means all the way to San Carlos?"

Stone Face nodded.

"Tell him to come on. I will do that."

"Good. We come." Stone Face rose and left into the night.

"Well? What now?"

"They're coming."

She hugged him. Only then did he realize she was naked.

26

Gray Fox led them riding the same fancy sorrel horse Geronimo had come in on to meet him. He looked as proud as he had the day they saw him at the stage stop. Sun rays gleamed on his bare skin and the eagle feather he wore in his hair twisted and turned in the cool morning breeze.

"Good morning," Slocum said as the two dozen riders gathered behind him.

"Good morning. I bring you a gift from Geronimo." Gray Fox drew his leg up and slid out of the saddle. He handed him the balled up cloth item.

Slocum shook it open and decided it was a shirt for a big man—a part of a *federales* uniform at that. Then he discovered the chevrons on the sleeve. He glanced up at Fox.

"He is no more."

"Good," Slocum said and looked hard at the garment. "The woman?"

"Ransomed. She is back at her father's hacienda."

"You seen Curly Madison?"

Fox made a face like he didn't know who he spoke about.

"Whiskey Man," Hawk said.

"No." Fox shook his head.

"Is that Franco's shirt?" Billie asked.

Slocum handed it to her. "He's dead, they say."

"You don't believe them?"

"I don't feel somehow it's over." He turned back to Fox. "You and I should go meet Captain Blake. He leads the black soldiers."

183

"Let us meet him." Fox turned and shouted something in Apache and the short warrior from the night before, Stone Face, joined him.

"Hawk," Slocum said. "You direct things for Billie and get them to help butcher and cook one of those steers today. But I don't want it all gritty with dirt. I've eaten in the camps of some bucks and their ideas about butchering are different from mine."

"We can string him up in a cottonwood," she said.

"I know, but they are used to eating on the go, and butchering the same way. I want this cooked so the black soldiers and Apaches can eat it here late this afternoon until they bust."

"We'll need to cut the meat up, then cook it in that short a time," she said, taking charge. "Hawk, send about three-fourths of them after firewood. We'll need lots of it."

"I'll be back," Slocum said and went for his horse.

Things were hurried from there. Fox and Captain Blake met and agreed to eat the beef together that evening. Sergeant Washington acted excited over the idea.

"That sure might relax us all," the big man said.

So with plans to leave in a day for Crystal Springs, Fox and Slocum rode away from the soldier's camp.

"You and Geronimo disagreed about this business of coming back?" Slocum asked Fox as they rode down the San Pedro bottoms under the great cottonwoods.

"He is a powerful man and sees many things in the future."

"I agree. But you don't see the same."

"I see children hungry. I see dead babies and bloody children. I see no victory dances, only crying wives."

Slocum nodded. There was no need to continue for his part. Gray Fox had spoken his heart.

A week later, Slocum and Billie rode back from San Carlos to the stage stop. It was a long hot dusty ride to the Webber's Spring stage stop. They dismounted at the porch and hitched their horses.

"Well, if it ain't ole Slocum hisself," Posey said, coming out in his red underwear top and britches to greet them.

"It's me," Slocum said. "Billie needs a bath."

"Rosie, this lady out here needs a bath." The stage man chuckled. "Guess she's a lady. I figured her for a boy when she showed up here a month ago."

"She's a lady all right." Slocum dropped out of the saddle and winced. His feet might never be the same again. He loosened the leather latigoes and arched his stiff back muscles—damn he was tired.

"When's the next stage west?" he asked.

"Oh, six hours."

"Eastbound?"

"Ah, four. Got more damn work to do today."

"Which way do you want a ticket for?" Slocum asked her.

"I ain't sure, yet." She took a bundle of her clothes under her arm and rushed inside.

Posey shouted to his help, two Mexican boys sitting in the shade. "Make damn sure them horses are ready." Then he turned back. "I've got a little whiskey inside. Let's have a shot and you can tell me all about this Apache business. I've been hearing bits and pieces of it."

Slocum took off his hat and wiped his wet forehead on his sleeve. "You're treating, I'm telling."

Over a short glass of whiskey, he told the stage station keeper all about his adventure—parts of it anyway. Just as he was concluding the story, Billie came out of the kitchen in her skirt and blouse outfit and Posey about swallowed his tongue.

"Who is this?"

"That boy," Slocum said and laughed.

"It can't be—"

Both men whirled at the challenge from outside.

"Get your ass out here, Slocum! I know you're in there. I come to kill you, you son of a bitch." It was Curly Madison.

"Don't—" She rushed over and blocked his way.

"My daddy always said, don't put off nothing."

"He ain't worth it."

Posey stood up and went for a double-barrel shotgun. "Use this on the dumb fucker. He needs killing." He set the scattergun on the table. "It's loaded."

"Slocum," she pleaded. "Don't—"

He removed the .44. Wished for a moment he had a better weapon, checked the caps on the nipples and satisfied, holstered it. "Stay in here," he said to her and headed for the door.

Madison's first shot plowed into the thick door frame beside

Slocum's head. It spooked the horses at the hitch rail. Slocum saw Madison duck behind a mud wagon. He fired twice at him, but knew neither shot had struck the ex-scout.

Then two doughnut blasts from the shooter behind the rig cut the air like angry hornets. Slocum answered with another and the fourth one was a misfire. He ran for the horses, holstered the Colt and jerked the .25/.20 single shot out of the scabbard.

He whirled around, drew the rifle to his shoulder, cocked the hammer back. His aim was centered on the chest of the angry-faced Madison coming around the wagon with his six-gun pointed at him. Slocum squeezed the trigger. The rifle spoke and Madison staggered two steps backward. His gun hand dropped and the look on his face went blank. He was dead before his knees buckled and spilled him facedown on the ground. His boots thrashed in the dust with the last throes of his life.

Slocum jammed the rifle in the scabbard and embraced the crying Billie who rushed out to be in his arms.

"It's over," he said.

He drew her in his arms and squeezed her tight.

Three hours later, he put Billie on the stage. He waved good-bye to her and it clattered off in the late afternoon. He went over and drew up the cinch on his saddle.

"Where you going next?" Posey asked, scratching his belly through the red underwear.

He stepped up in the stirrup, swung his leg over and nodded to the man. "Wherever the wind takes me." His right hand touched his hat brim and he rode off leading Billie's pony.

Watch for

SLOCUM AND THE HORSE KILLERS

329th novel in the exciting SLOCUM series

from Jove

Coming in July!